THE DEAD CAN TELL

The Persons this Mystery is about—

CRISTIE LANSING,
beautiful young artist from Texas, whose love of Steven Hazard has stood the test of a three-year separation.

STEVEN HAZARD,
a promising young engineer, who still loves Cristie although he is married to the dazzling Sara Hazard.

CHRISTOPHER McKEE,
the level-headed Scotsman, head of the Manhattan Homicide Squad, who uncovers the murderer although the trail is very cold.

TODHUNTER,
the mousey, indispensable little detective whom no one would glance at once, let alone twice.

MARY DODD,
intelligent, kindly spinster, a friend of both Sara and Steven Hazard.

MARGOT ST. VRAIN,
the Queen of Swing and the foremost band agent in the country, who shares a penthouse apartment with her cousin Johnny and her friend Cristie.

SARA HAZARD,
the gorgeous, golden-haired wife of Steven Hazard, with something ruthless and self-centered beneath her golden loveliness.

CLIFFORD SOMERS,
an assemblyman who has made a name for himself in politics through daring, courage, and a capacity for lying convincingly—plus a little push from his brother.

PAT SOMERS,
Clifford's brother, a real behind-the-scenes big shot who has helped put Clifford where he is.

EUEN FIRTH,
Margot's fiancé, who, being the son of a wealthy drug manufacturer, can give her the things she wants.

JOHNNY ST. VRAIN,
prominent radio announcer and cousin of Margot St. Vrain.

KIT BLAKETON,
Mary Dodd's red-haired, vivacious niece, engaged to Clifford Somers, who has lived with her aunt since Dr. Dodd died.

EVA PRENTICE,
the Hazards' maid, who is blond and good-looking, and listens at doors.

D1027337

THE DEAD CAN TELL

Things this Mystery is about—

An expensive ermine CLOAK . . .

An anonymous NOTE made up of cutout letters . . .

A gold COMPACT . . .

A black-handled GUN . . .

A thousand dollars in CASH . . .

A tinkling antique silver BRACELET . . .

The RECORD of a conversation . . .

A SPADE . . .

A· CHRISTOPHER McKEE DETECTIVE STORY

THE DEAD
CAN TELL

By HELEN REILLY

Author of "Death Demands an Audience,"
"Dead Man Control," "McKee of Centre Street," etc.

*All of the characters and incidents
in this novel are entirely imaginary*

DELL PUBLISHING COMPANY
George T. Delacorte, Jr., President   *Helen Meyer, Vice-President*
149 Madison Avenue
NEW YORK, N. Y.

THE DEAD CAN TELL

List of Exciting Chapters—

The Dead Can Tell

Chapter One
THE GIRL IN GRAY

ALL THAT Christopher McKee, the head of the Manhattan Homicide Squad, had when he started on that investigation were a remembered glimpse of two people in a café and an anonymous letter. He wasn't even in New York when the crime was committed. He was on his way to Rio de Janeiro where he had been sent by the Mayor at the special request of the Brazilian authorities.

Fernandez, New York's Chief Medical Examiner, slim, dark and elegant in sand color, and the Inspector, lean and towering in loose gray flannel, were having a cocktail in the El Capitan on East Sixty-third Street when Fernandez said with a grin, "Don't look now, McKee, but there's one of the prettiest girls I've ever seen right behind you. I know how interested you are in pretty girls."

McKee didn't turn. He said indifferently, "If Irving Berlin's right, your life must be one long sweet song. How many prettiest girls do you run into of a day? About that hydrocyanic—if it *is* there, why the five stab wounds?"

"By Jove," Fernandez said, "she is lovely. I didn't think they made them like that any more."

McKee glanced past three frosted mint juleps and an array of decorative bottles at the subject of Fernandez's appreciative gaze. He saw a slim girl in a gray linen dress with touches of raspberry and peacock at the throat and an absurd raspberry hat tilted over glinting chestnut haïr. Her white throat was arched. There was tension in her white profile, short straight nose, competent chin, sensitive mouth. The tension, the conflict, were repeated in her eyes, wide-set violet-gray eyes with depths to them, set at a tilt under delicate dark brows.

"Ah!" Fernandez murmured, "the incriminating document."

The girl had taken a note out of her purse and was reading it. Her slight figure was erect. There was a haunted look in the violet-gray eyes.

McKee finished his ale.

"Ready?" Fernandez asked regretfully.

"No," the Scotsman answered, "I'm going to have another." He pushed his glass toward the bartender and kept on looking into the mirror.

The girl in gray didn't notice the two men at the bar. Outside, the blazing August afternoon was breathless, the interior of the café was cool, dim. She had slipped into the first unoccupied booth near the door. She was shaking a little. There was haze all about her. She told herself she shouldn't have come, shouldn't have given in, no matter what Steve said. To meet like this was stupid, dangerous, would only get them into more trouble. It was lunacy. They were rational human beings. She was twenty-six and Steven was thirty-two. If those weren't years of discretion, when did you reach them? In your second childhood?

It was wrong, all wrong, not only to themselves but to another human being, no matter what sort of person that other human being was. Cristie Lansing lit a cigarette with quick nervous movements and read Steve's note again.

Cristie: I've got to see you. Something tremendous has come up. Meet me without fail at five this afternoon at El Capitan.

A waiter paused beside the booth. Cristie shook her head slightly, started to return the note to her purse and changed her mind. Better tear it up.

She and Steven had had their chance and they had thrown it away. That was three years ago. They had quarreled and busted it up. The quarrel between them had been childish, silly, meaningless. She couldn't even remember now what it had been about. Pride, obstinacy, hot temper, wounded vanity had prevented either of them from making the first move. So no move was made and she had gone back to Texas with her defeated hopes and absurd canvases and her heartache and Steven had married another woman.

Steven had a wife. There was no getting away from that.

She went on reducing the sheet of paper to lozenges and squares. Simply because she and Steven had met again here in New York at the beginning of August and she had been weak enough, foolish enough to see Steve three times since that first accidental meeting was no good reason for cracking up Steven's career, Sara's life and her own.

She had built up a new existence for herself, slowly and laboriously—had her work. Not the creation of the gigantic murals that had occupied her during those long-ago days when she and Steven had gone around together, young and happy and in love with each other and with life, but pen-and-ink sketches that had caught on and were bringing her in a good price and were fun to do.

It was during their last meeting that she had discovered that the past wasn't dead and that the feeling they had for each other, instead of weakening with time, had taken on a new fire and a depth that threatened to sweep them both off their feet.

It was she who had called the turn. The thing between herself and Steven was too fine for muddling, for shabbiness and intrigue and hypocrisy and deceit. Scraps and fragments weren't of any use. There was no middle ground. It was all or nothing. It couldn't be all. It had to be nothing. Steven was married and had a wife. You couldn't do that to another woman. It wasn't decent or honorable or fair.

As soon as she realized what had happened she had taken steps. She had been quite frank, keeping emotion out of it, on the surface, at any rate. She could go back and pick out the very bush in Central Park beside which she had halted when she said, "Look, Steve, you'd better go. Now. Yes, I admit it, I find myself liking you again too much, thinking about you too much for my own peace of mind. I thought it was gone, that I was—free. But I'm not. So will you ... ?"

Steven had said good-bye huskily, abruptly, after a short volcanic protest, and they had agreed not to meet again. It was over and the pain was beginning to recede, to dull just a little—and then he had asked her to meet him, and here she was.

Flight was still possible. Cristie glanced at the clock. He had said five and it was only just that. If she went now, quickly—she measured the distance to the street, and her heart took a leap, a leap that was half joy and half foreboding. Steve was coming toward her along the aisle, tall, wide-shouldered, with that familiar swing, cocked dark head at a go-to-hell angle, keen, steel-colored eyes alight in his long clever face.

He reached the table, paused beside it. "Cristie!"

His voice had a triumphant lift to it. It was forceful and eager and decisive. He threw himself down on the white leather cushions opposite, reached out and took her two hands in his. It wasn't right, couldn't lead anywhere but to pain and frustration and sorrow and regret. The blood tingled through Cristie's veins, put a rose flush in her slender cheeks and a glow into the lovely eyes in pools of shadow made by the lashes. An electric fan blew a wisp of soft hair across her white forehead.

"Steve, what is it?" she demanded. "What's happened?" Thoughts dashed helter-skelter through her mind. Was it something about Sara? What *could* it be?

Steven said, "I knew it would work out, Cristie. I knew there was a way. I've found it."

Cristie caught her breath. "What way, Steve?"

Steven said, "If I take the Argentine laboratory, and Wilbur put it up to me directly this afternoon, yes or no, then don't you see, Cristie ... ?"

Cristie didn't see. Sara was still there, she was still be-
· tween them. There was no international date-line on a marriage. You couldn't get unmarried by crossing a border. "But, Steve, what about Sara?"

Lines etched themselves suddenly around Steven's mouth. It lost its resilience; it was wry, a little sad. He said soberly, "Don't worry about Sara, Cristie. You don't have to. That's the point."

Cristie withdrew her hands from his. She said stiffly, "But I *do* worry, Steven. I have to worry. You can't get what you want by grabbing, by stealing from someone else, making someone else unhappy. You're Sara's husband, and

Sara's your wife. I'm a woman too. I wouldn't want another woman to do that to me. It's dishonest and greedy and unfair."

Steven nodded. He reached for her cold fingers, imprisoned them in his. "I know what you mean, Cristie, but I don't think you quite understand. God knows I tried to make a go of it with Sara, tried to make her happy. The whole thing was wrong from the beginning. I should never have married her. Once it was done, I did everything in my power to make our marriage a success. That sounds as though I'm excusing myself, but I'm not. It's the truth." His mouth took a grim twist.

Cristie looked at him. She didn't say anything. Steven had always been a scrupulous person.

He went on, "Sara never loved me either. Whatever little feeling she had wore off after the first few months. She's not happy with me. I can't give her the things she wants, the only sort of life she really craves. She's suggested herself, at least twice, that we call it a day. She was the one who mentioned the word 'divorce' first."

A pulse in Cristie's throat beat in and out. "Divorce!"

"Yes," Steven said firmly, "divorce. She spoke of one a year ago. National Motors wanted me to take the Argentine laboratory then. It was the opportunity I was after. No engineer could ask for a better. The equipment's tip-top. It would have given me a fine chance for experimental work. But Sara absolutely refused to go. She said she'd divorce me if I accepted the post, and now, well—don't you see?"

This time Cristie did see. Her defenses began to crumble. If Sara didn't love Steven, if she was willing to divorce him, wanted a divorce herself . . .

Steven leaned across the table. He was closer to her. His words came faster. "Don't worry about Sara. Sara will agree. I know she will, like a shot, when I make my offer. She wouldn't dream of leaving New York and her tight little world. She doesn't care a snap of her fingers for me, doesn't want anything from me except cold cash. It may be a little hard for us for a while, darling. Sara will demand everything. It will mean a commitment for big alimony. But it will be worth it. Think of it, Cristie. We can wipe out that miserable blunder we made three years ago. We can start over again."

To start over again, with Steven, in South America. New horizons and a new existence—together. The thought of it shook Cristie almost unbearably. She lowered her lashes to hide the flame that had sprung up in her eyes, tried to drag herself back to sanity. There were a lot of obstacles to be surmounted. And yet...Steven's voice was in her ears.

"Look at me, darling."

Cristie raised her lashes slowly.

At the bar McKee turned. He glanced at the girl's radiant face lifted to the man on the other side of the table. Strong emotion can be as tangible as a breeze, a shout. It was there in those two people. It hadn't been there a moment before. He couldn't hear what they were saying. He didn't need to hear. We hold these truths to be self-evident.

Twenty feet away Steven Hazard was repeating softly, "So you see it's going to be all right if—love me, Cristie?"

This time it was Cristie's hands that found his. She touched the back of Steven's with the tips of her fingers. "You know, don't you?" she whispered.

There was no hesitation in her answer. But she was still

not completely convinced. Could you ever go back and wipe out the past? Steven sensed her uncertainty, because he said with sudden iron in his voice, "You don't know what my marriage is like. You don't know it at all, Cristie. I'm not going to go into it. But we're entitled to another chance, you and I. It isn't as though I were welching on Sara. She doesn't want me, doesn't want any part of me. Our life together is over. If she gets money enough it will suit her down to the ground to let me go. That's all I can tell you."

His brooding gaze left Cristie for a moment, he was far away, enclosed in the shadows of a dark inward knowledge. He straightened his wide shoulders like a man shaking himself free of a physical weight. His eyes cleared. His muscles relaxed. He said forcefully, "I'm going straight home. I'm going to put it up to Sara, now, at once, today. And tonight at Margot St. Vrain's party, when the decks are clear, we'll be able to make our plans, definite plans."

Happiness should have been singing through Cristie. The happiness was there but there were other things mixed up with it.

"Sara won't be with you?" she said. "Margot asked her."

"No," Steven replied, signaling to the waiter. He ordered cocktails. "'Sara's going to the opening of 'The Star-spangled Manner' with the Johnsons."

The cocktails were brought. "To us," Steven said, raising his glass.

Their eyes met and held. A wave of joy engulfed Cristie. She stopped fighting, let it take her. They kept on looking at each other.

Cristie had come to New York from Texas late in the

spring, after her mother's death. She was staying for the summer with Margot St. Vrain in Margot's penthouse on East Sixty-fourth Street. Margot's people had been friends of Cristie's father. Margot and Margot's cousin, Johnny St. Vrain, the radio announcer, had been in Texas when her mother died and they had both pressed her to come north. It was Margot who had fallen on Cristie's pen-and-ink sketches with a scream of delight, Margot who had made her send them around. They had had an almost immediate, if modest, success.

Steven left Cristie at the door of Margot's apartment. Her mood of exhilaration began to fade as he walked away. Entering the lobby, going up in the small private elevator that serviced the penthouse, the doubts and tremors and questions began to come back. Granting that Sara wanted a divorce herself, would she make some impossible conditions? Cristie tried to push her fears aside; they refused to go, completely.

When she went into the penthouse living room, Margot was there, with Euen Firth, the man Margot was engaged to, and so was Johnny. Cristie said hello to Margot, tall and competent and square in a superbly cut, brown shantung coat and skirt that intensified her height and leanness and brought out the lines of a magnificent pair of shoulders and arms. They were Margot's one really good point and she made the most of them.

Johnny waved a cheerful greeting to Cristie as she pulled off her hat and settled down in a corner of the immense geranium-red sofa. Looking at Johnny's shapely head, his compact body, his pleasant handsome face, listening to his voice, a voice that even in a room had the ring to it that had put him well at the top of America's leading announcers, Cristie knew why she hadn't married him when he had asked her in the spring. It was because he wasn't Steven. Her refusal hadn't made any difference in the camaraderie between herself and the St. Vrains. She had been afraid it would, but it hadn't.

Margot's engagement to Euen Firth had been announced in the morning papers. They were discussing plans and a date. Margot said firmly that she couldn't leave New York until after Thanksgiving. Two or three pots were due to boil in late November and she had to be on deck to watch the proceedings.

Cristie looked at her wistfully. Margot was so sure of herself. At thirty-one she was the foremost band agent in the country, and she had started from scratch. Left with an illustrious name and nothing with which to back it up, she had gradually built a business that was the despair of her competitors. "You've got to see St. V. to swing" had become an axiom among the jive and jam folk. Winchell had called Margot the Queen of Swing in a Sunday night broadcast.

But Cristie knew that although Margot's income was large, her expenses were high and the pace was terrific. She had engaged herself to Euen Firth with her eyes open, made no secret of it. She wasn't and she didn't pretend to be, madly in love with the gangling, not quite "ex." playboy in his early thirties, with a prospective couple of millions in his jeans. Euen was the son of Charles Firth, one of the country's leading drug manufacturers. Not that Margot wasn't fond of Euen in her own way. She was, but she had explained to Cristie quite frankly that he could give her the things she wanted, the chance to stop and take a deep breath, to lie back and relax and laze a bit—for a while, anyhow.

Margot went on talking, but she gave Cristie a shrewd glance. Cristie averted her face. The gnawing little worm of fear in her breast stirred. Margot was terrifically keen, saw all there was to see. She didn't know, specifically, about Steven. Cristie didn't want her to know, didn't want anyone to know—yet.

She was relieved when the maid entered and said that Margot was wanted on the phone. Cristie wasn't afraid of Johnny or of Euen. Men didn't notice things, like women. Johnny went on reading the lyric of a new Harry Woods song and sipping a Tom Collins. Euen was engrossed in a newspaper.

Margot was away for about five minutes. When she re-entered the living room, a modernistic room mollified by incongruous and comfortable additions that would have driven its designer mad, a change had come over her. Her mouth was constricted and her strong plain face was a bad color. Johnny put his feet, flung over a chair, on the floor.

"Who was it, Margot?" he asked, frowning at his cousin.

At Margot's answer the blood rushed into Cristie's face, stained her throat. Standing near a table, rolling a cigarette between the fingers of a large shapely hand, Margot said in a queer flat tone, "It was Steven Hazard's wife, Sara." The cigarette she was holding broke and tobacco dribbled to the floor.

Cristie was aware of the fact that Margot knew Sara. They had been at Miss Brandon's school together, and Sara had been a pupil there when Margot was teaching deportment for room and board and nothing a year before she started her upward climb. The connection between them was neither close nor intimate. Cristie's hands tightened in her lap. What had Sara Hazard said to Margot to make her look like that? Something disturbing, certainly.

Margot threw the ruined cigarette into the waste basket, got another from a box, lit it and said, without turning to Euen Firth, lolling in his corner with a highball, "Sara Hazard mentioned you on the phone just now, Euen. I didn't know you were a friend of hers."

A surge of relief, a dart of surprise, wonder; it was then that it began for Cristie, that baffling sense of distortion, of values superimposed on other values, the underlying ones quite different from those that showed on top.

Euen Firth blinked sandy lashes. His eyes were uneasy, furtive. "Sara Hazard...? Who the hell is Sara...?" His long, sallow, high-nosed face and dish-chin smoothed themselves out. "That's right," he said, "I remember now. Yes. I met a Mrs. Hazard at the Jettison's on Long Island last winter."

He got up and helped himself to a fistful of Scotch and very little vichy. His narrow-shouldered back was turned. He forgot to release the siphon on the bottle and the vichy squirted over the tray in a wide pool.

The other two didn't notice, but Cristie did. Margot was looking at Johnny. It was a strange look, weighing, speculative. Cristie was conscious of a slight feeling of suffocation. Johnny didn't meet Margot's glance. He was gazing out at the terrace with its hedge of cedars in red terra-cotta pots against the broken frieze of the towers of New York and a mauve evening sky barred with long streaks of green.

There was a funny little pause. Nobody said anything. Then Johnny said with a yawn, "I don't like that woman. I ran into her the other day with the Henleys. I don't care how long it is before I see her again."

Margot was crossing to her desk, a chromium and leather contraption with half a hundred drawers. She seated herself, took out a memorandum book and said over her shoulder, "Oh, but you will, Johnny, darling. You and Euen will both see her, shortly. She wasn't coming to my party tonight. She's changed her mind." He intonation was clipped, incisive.

Euen's highball halted halfway to his lips. Johnny's brows drew together. Cristie saw them both through a mist. Her sense of foreboding, her latent fear had quickened, sharply. Steven had said that Sara was going to the theater with friends. Why had she altered her plans? What did it mean? Cristie felt herself beginning to shake.

She got up, walked to one of the windows and stood there with her back turned, looking out into the dusk.

Chapter Two
THE ERMINE CAPE

WITH the coming of darkness Cristie's spirits lifted. The atmosphere of the penthouse helped. It was anticipative, brisk, and every moment was bringing her nearer to Steven. Margot had thrown off her preoccupation and was busy with a thousand details. Sara Hazard's name wasn't mentioned again. Cristie tried to forget her. At seven Euen and Johnny went home to change and Margot and Cristie had a quiet meal together, just a bite because the dining room was filled with the caterer and his men.

Cristie dressed quickly, slashing herself to renewed vigor with a hot and cold shower. Eau de Cologne, a mist of powder, cobwebs of stockings, white sandals. She applied lipstick and slid into cool white chiffon, yards and yards of it, bound round her midriff with a girdle of silver.

Margot wore stiff, sweeping brown net that was superlatively smart and reduced mere prettiness to a wishy-washy non-essential. She had invited almost a hundred guests. Publicity was good for her business. Cristie got a fleeting impression once or twice in those last moments that she would have liked to call the whole thing off. There was nothing solid to tie it to.

People began arriving at around half past nine. By half past ten the spacious, flower-decked rooms were well filled. There was music, sweet and swing. There was dancing. There were games. There was impromptu singing. Voices were recorded on a special machine that Margot had for her composers. A number of the guests had a try at it and there were exclamations of dismay and corresponding laughter when the records were played back. A new baritone from the Met sang and there was a soft-shoe dance by Gorkin from the town's hit musical.

Men in white jackets and women in thin, colorful gowns wandered into every room and out on the terrace. The drinks were plentiful and excellent. Euen Firth, tall and sandy and beaming, was in his element as auxiliary bar man. He was one of his own best customers.

As the evening advanced and the time she might expect to see Steven approached, the penthouse began to be peopled with shadows as far as Cristie was concerned. Smile, reply, respond to talk—about the weather, about how well Margot was looking, about what a splendid fellow Euen Firth was. Her whole being was centered on the thought of Steven, when he would come and what he would have to tell her.

She tried to banish Sara and her belated telephone call, tried not to speculate as to why Sara had given up the theater and was coming to the penthouse instead. The attempt wasn't a success. She wasn't the only one who was troubled. She hadn't imagined it; there had been something peculiar about the way Margot and Johnny and Euen had reacted to Sara's shift in plans. Perhaps it was to see or say something to one of them, that she was coming.

Cristie was standing beside Margot in the long and wide hall that ran from the foyer to glass doors opening on the terrace in back when Miss Dodd arrived. The daughter of the eminent psychologist was a friend of Steven's. Steven was very fond of her; had spoken more than once of her intelligence, her understanding. Tragedy had touched her early. She had seen her fiancé killed in an accident before her eyes when she was a girl. Mary Dodd had gone to school with Sara Hazard's oldest sister and had known Sara from childhood, but she was Steven's friend too.

She was a tall woman in her middle thirties with an interesting face, not beautiful, her nose was too long for beauty, her forehead was too high, but there was dignity in her supple figure, sensitiveness in her thin, fine-boned hands and her clear hazel eyes were youthful. A streak of white running through her thick dark hair added to her air of distinction. She wore black that brought out the fresh tones of her skin.

When Margot introduced them, Mary Dodd shook Cristie's hand warmly. She said she had seen Cristie's pen-and-ink drawings in the *New Yorker* and told her how much she liked them.

Cristie was pleased. She said deprecatingly that they were silly little things.

Margot said, "Don't let her kid you, Miss Dodd. It's swell stuff and she's going places with it."

Miss Dodd wanted her niece, Kit Blaketon, to meet Cristie. She disentangled a girl in green from a laughing group. Kit Blaketon was lithe, slender-waisted, long-legged. Red hair in a long page-boy bob flamed away from a thin face with a pointed chin and an enormous pair of bright green eyes.

Kit Blaketon was of no particular interest to Cristie then. Kit had lived with Mary Dodd since the death of Miss Dodd's father a year and a half earlier, was engaged to a man named Cliff. She gave Cristie a perfunctory smile, said to Margot, "Darling of you to have us. I'm mad about

Gorkin. Do wangle it so I get a dance with him later."
A young man touched her shoulder and she waltzed off,
humming the refrain of a popular song.

Mary Dodd and Margot were talking. Cristie took a
stout woman in pink velvet in tow, showed her where to
put her wraps, abandoned her. Why didn't Steven come?
It was almost eleven. Her throat was tight. Could he have
come in when she wasn't watching? She kept looking
anxiously through the throngs on the terrace. He was
nowhere in sight. What *could* be keeping him? The pros-
pect of his arrival made her feel light-headed. At the same
time there was a cold little core of fear at the heart of her
expectation that wouldn't dissolve.

She had almost forgotten about Sara Hazard. And suddenly she saw her. Cristie stood where she was in the
partial shelter of a tall sheaf of gladiolas. Her hands, hanging at her sides, were hidden in folds of white chiffon. The
fingers were tightly clenched.

Sara Hazard's entrance into the party at the penthouse
that night was, as always, spectacular. Three steps led down
from the hall above. She paused on the top step and looked
around. Cristie wasn't the only one who stared.

Sara Hazard had a picture sense where her extremely
attractive body was concerned, managed to make you aware
of it, in some subtle fashion, even when she was standing
still. Perhaps her own concentration with it had something
to do with the effect she contrived to produce.

The word slim covers a lot of territory. Sara was slim
enough but there were curves, the right curves in the right
places. She wore a daringly brief evening gown of black
and gold that left practically nothing unsaid. Her upthrust
breast had the pout of invitation to it and the gently swell-

ing hips under the gold corselet that defined the small waist seemed, in spite of her immobility, to sway a little.

Her golden hair, hair that was really golden, was turned back from her long narrow white face in a soft roll. Everything about her was narrow, velvet-brown eyes, straight nose, hands and feet, everything except her mouth. Her mouth was a full scarlet bow. The lower lip, a Hapsburg, was inclined to protrude a little. You didn't notice it at first. The general effect was too good.

Sara Hazard was alone.

Cristie's eyes absorbed the emptiness beside and behind her as Sara descended to the floor, located Margot and strolled in Margot's direction. Heads turned as she passed and people stared, women with a touch of envy, men with admiration and here and there something rather more intense.

Cristie stayed where she was, conflicting emotions driving to and fro inside of her. How could Steven care for her when he had such a beautiful wife—because Sara Hazard was very, very beautiful; there could be no two opinions about that. But Cristie's critical faculties hadn't deserted her. There was something self-centered, ruthless, beneath that smooth golden exterior, that lift of long-lashed white lids, the poise of the small gold head. The implication of cruelty was there. She must have made Steven suffer. Cristie understood now why he had spoken of her as he had that afternoon.

Sara was in the middle of a knot of men. There was ferment around her, the stir of raised voices, laughter. There would be. There were other women like that, women who were insatiably vain, who knew the conventions of decent living thoroughly and who used them or cast them aside as it suited their purpose. They were women with the morality of emotional Al Capones. Danger was their natural orbit. Sara Hazard vanished in the crowd. Still no Steven. What could be keeping him?

Cristie was standing in the shadowy embrasure of a window trying to reassure herself, telling herself not to be an idiot, when two women halted on the terrace just outside.

"—but I've only got one life to live. What a woman's husband doesn't know is her own business."

Cristie turned her head. The light metallic voice was Sara Hazard's. Mary Dodd was with her. The latter's recoil was thinly veiled. Her tall figure was drawn up and she was gazing with displeasure at the lovely, narrow, closed white face looking intently into her own.

Cristie wanted to move, to get away from that voice. She didn't. The next moment she wished she had. Sara Hazard paused, then it came out with a rush. Fingers busy with a gold cigarette case, smooth head bent, she said abruptly, "Mary, can you loan me some money?"

Mary Dodd didn't answer for a moment. Then she said a little wearily, "Same old thing, I suppose, Sara. Bills again?"

Sara Hazard struck a match. "Rather—and then some. A man from Prince and Consort's actually had the impudence to force his way into the apartment this morning and demand a thousand dollars on account immediately— or else. Can you imagine the nerve? There was nothing I could do with him. Heaven knows I tried." She put the match to the tip of a cigarette. Her thin sinuous lips were curved in a smile. "Anyhow, Mary, the long and short of it is, I've got to produce right away or I'm sunk, irrevocably and irretrievably sunk."

Mary Dodd said slowly, not looking at her companion, "And Steven doesn't know, I presume. How much do you really have to have, Sara?"

Sara Hazard flicked ash from the gold embroidery clasping her white breast. "I've got to have the whole thousand, Mary."

Mary Dodd said firmly, "It's impossible, Sara. I haven't got more than a few hundred in the bank and it will be a couple of weeks before my regular checks come in."

Sara Hazard turned so that her face was fully illuminated by shafting brightness from a battery of lamps over the piano. Her nostrils were flaring. "Sweetness and light, aren't you, Mary," she drawled, "except when it comes to the draw. You can't give me anything but love, baby."

Miss Dodd flinched. She was white. She was about to make an angry rejoinder when a couple ambled in her direction followed by a tall man with a beard and a paper cap on. Cristie was glad she didn't have to listen to any more. Bills, mountains of them apparently, and Steven didn't know. What else was there that Steven didn't know? But perhaps he did. Perhaps that was what he had meant when he said there were things he couldn't tell her. Cristie shook out folds of white chiffon. Over and above the trouble Sara could still cause Steven, she didn't like the complications that were cropping up, tangled threads whose ends she couldn't see.

She turned instinctively in a movement toward escape. Two people blocked her way. As she edged around them, the voices of the two women outside followed her. Sara Hazard asked a question about "Cliff." Cliff was the name of the man Miss Dodd's niece, Kit Blaketon, was engaged to. Mary Dodd said something about the "Penobscott Club" and "eleven or twelve."

Cristie was to recall that later. She danced with Euen and then with Johnny, spoke to Margot who looked rather pale in spite of fresh lipstick and rouge. Margot was tired.

Then she ran into Sara Hazard again, or rather didn't run into her, because her place, the place of unseen observer, had been taken by someone else. Cristie was crossing the hall in the direction of her own bedroom for fresh powder when she turned the corner and stood still. Her bedroom door was open. Sara Hazard was seated at her desk. She was at the telephone. Her voice was low but the desk was close to the door and Cristie heard her say, "Penobscott Club?" And then she didn't hear any more. Her attention changed its focus.

There was a girl standing between herself and Sara Hazard, a girl in green with flaming red hair. The girl was Kit Blaketon, Miss Dodd's niece. Kit Blaketon's face was hidden but there was no mistaking the tension, the stress in the slim body pressed against wall and door jamb. She was invisible from inside the room. She was listening to what Sara Hazard was saying over the telephone.

Cristie drew back, walked away, returned to the living room. She had only just reached it when she saw Sara Hazard leave the hall and go out into the foyer. She was wearing the gold jacket that was part of her gown but she had no wrap on. She had scarcely disappeared from view when the red-haired Kit Blaketon went through the foyer doors in turn. She was carrying a green velvet coat over her arm. Something about the girl's swift progress suggested a stalking. Was she—could she possibly be trailing the other woman? Cristie watched the doors for some time. Neither of the two returned. She forgot them in her increasing tension about Steven.

It was getting late, he must know that she would be anxious, would be waiting. She exhorted herself to patience. There were a lot of things he might have to do. It wasn't nearly midnight yet. The party was still in its first flight. The din was continuous. Cristie listened to the music for a while, had a scotch and soda with Euen Firth and heard an interminable story with some vague point which Euen didn't seem to have quite clear.

The noise, the stir, the incessant merriment began to get on her nerves. They were raw and taut and the discord was like the rasping of a giant file. Her longing to see Steven, to know that he was all right, to know that everything was all right, was like thirst. Her cheeks were burning and her eyes were tired from the colored lights.

She evaded two partners, young friends of Margot's, went out on the terrace and around to the far side. It was quieter there and cool and dim. She was leaning against the railing at the southern end with her back to the city below when she saw Sara Hazard enter Margot's bedroom.

Sara Hazard went to Margot's dressing table, put her purse down, took off the tight-fitting gold jacket, powdered her face, neck and arms and applied fresh lipstick. She scrutinized her face carefully in the mirror, retrieved the jacket and purse. It was a big, black velvet purse with gold corners and her monogram in gold on the front. Cristie thought she was going to leave the room but she didn't.

The raised bed was loaded with wraps. Sara Hazard's wasn't among them. Her cape of summer ermine was thrown over a chair in a recess beyond the bed. She crossed to the recess, paused beside the chair and opened her purse.

Cristie stared. She straightened. The blood drained out of her face and from her heart.

Sara Hazard's movements were swift. There was no mistaking them or the thing, the object, she removed from the purse and dropped into a capacious pocket of the ermine cape. Light from the lamp glinted on it as it disappeared from sight. It was a small, squat, black pistol.

Sara Hazard had a gun with her, a gun that she was shifting around, a gun that she didn't want anyone to know about.

Chapter Three
No Longer There

CRISTIE DIDN'T know what to do. Margot was her first thought, but Margot was in the dining room with Euen's father and mother. She couldn't very well interrupt them with a bald announcement that one of the guests had a gun. If only Steven would come! She sat down on a chair in a deserted row in the living room. She was glad to be back where there were lights and laughter and people. The darkness had been terrifying.

A man hurrying past paused in front of her. It was Johnny. Cristie tried to smile up at him but the presence of that ugly black weapon hidden in the silk-lined pocket of the ermine cape in the bedroom beyond was a weight, a question, dragging her down, putting pallor into her cheeks, stiffness into her vocal cords.

Johnny didn't notice her condition. He said, "Seen anything of Sara Hazard, Cristie? I'm looking for her."

He didn't say why. Cristie looked at him dumbly. Why was Johnny so anxious as to Sara's whereabouts when he had announced his dislike of her only a few hours ago? Cristie felt as though she were treading a slow measure of nightmare with the golden figure of Sara Hazard appearing and disappearing in its coils. She was the object of a peculiar attention on the part of Margot, Johnny, Euen, and Kit Blaketon, an attention all the more striking because none of them seemed to care for her. Johnny appeared to sense her unspoken query. He said vaguely that someone wanted Sara Hazard on the phone.

Cristie told him that Sara was or had been in Margot's bedroom a few minutes earlier.

"That's funny," Johnny said, "I looked there before."

Cristie said coldly, "Mrs. Hazard left here, went out somewhere a while ago. But she's back."

"Sure, Cristie?"

"Quite sure." If only she weren't so sure of what she had seen from the darkness of the terrace!

Johnny left her without another word. He made for the study and the telephone there. Cristie's perplexity thickened. Why didn't Johnny find Sara Hazard and take her to the telephone instead of going back to it himself? She brushed the cobwebby incongruities aside only to have them crop out in another place.

Sara Hazard wasn't the only person being sought in that maze of people at Margot's engagement party. Mary Dodd was hunting for her niece. She looked worried. Cristie heard her inquiring about the lithe, red-haired girl with the green eyes. She got out of her chair, went to Miss Dodd and told her about Kit Blaketon's departure.

Cristie said, "She left some time ago. She may have returned, though. Can I help?"

Before Mary Dodd could reply a man joined them. Mary murmured his name. He was Clifford Somers, Assemblyman Clifford Somers, the man Kit Blaketon was engaged to. He was a well-set-up young fellow of twenty-eight or so with a pleasant, likeable face, a good jaw, and straightforward blue eyes. Cristie knew who he was then. She had heard Margot speak of him.

Clifford Somers had made a name for himself in politics.

He was talked of for bigger things than the Assembly. Part of his success was the result of his own ability, but part of it was due to the influence of his brother Pat.

Steven and Margot had both talked to Pat Somers. He was one of the most powerful men in New York. He never figured in the news but he was one of the real behind-the-scenes big shots. Pat knew everybody and went every place. Cristie had met him. He had been at the penthouse for dinner when she first came.

Clifford Somers was talking to Mary Dodd. He said, "I hope she's not sore, Mary. Where is she? It was hard breaking away from the Penobscott Club. I thought the speeches would never end. But I had to sit through it. I'm running this year, you know, and I've got to mind my p's and q's."

His face fell when Mary Dodd told him that Kit wasn't there. "I hoped she was with you, Cliff. Miss Lansing saw her go out a while ago. Was she alone, Miss Lansing?"

Cristie hesitated. The Penobscott Club. Queer. That was the place Sara Hazard was calling when Kit Blaketon was listening to her outside the door. Ought she to tell Mary Dodd privately what she had seen and heard? She decided against it. She might be making a mountain out of a mole-hill and, anyhow, it wasn't any of her business.

She said aloud, "Yes, Miss Blaketon was alone, but she had her coat with her."

Mary Dodd said hopefully, "She may have run over to the Turners for a few minutes, Cliff. They live near here. She'll probably turn up. She wouldn't go for good without letting me know. Where's Pat, Cliff? I thought he was coming tonight."

Cliff Somers's eyes were roaming the crowd absently. "Pat? No, Pat couldn't make it. He meant to, but he had to go to Albany to have a talk with the Governor and he wouldn't be back until tomorrow."

Mary Dodd and the young Assemblyman moved toward the supper room. The party was at its peak. It was a decided success, but then it would be with Margot running it. In spite of her temporary absence, Sara Hazard was very much in evidence. She seemed to be everywhere. She was very gay. Other people besides Cristie watched her that night.

Sara chatted with Margot, rumbaed with Euen Firth, had champagne with Johnny. Toward twelve o'clock she did a solo with Gorkin, the dancer. The rest of the room was darkened and a spotlight played over them. Sara's black-sheathed figure with its small golden head swayed and twisted in perfect time with the musical comedy star's.

Watching from the sidelines, Cristie kept telling herself that it wasn't really very late, not much after midnight. There was plenty of time. Steven would be there soon. And then she saw him.

It was as the applause broke out and the lights flashed on again that Steven arrived. The width of the room and sixty or seventy people separated him from Cristie. She had only a glimpse of him beyond the door into the hall, wide-shouldered, lean, dark head high. The glimpse was too swift to tell her anything as she started across the floor.

It wasn't until more than half an hour later that they found themselves alone together on the terrace. The night was warm with a soft wind. There were no stars. It was very dark. The millions of electric bulbs in the city spread out at their feet and the illuminated windows of the penthouse supplied light enough. Cristie knew what Steven was going to tell her before he spoke, had somehow, she realized dully, known it all along. Sara wasn't going to give him a divorce.

Steven stood beside and a little behind Cristie. He was rigid as though part of him were somewhere else. He didn't attempt to touch her. He stared straight in front of him into blackness as he said in a hard cold voice, a voice without cadences, without inflection, "She won't do it, Cristie. Sara won't give me a divorce. She won't let me go."

Cristie took it standing up, gripping the railing with her hands. She looked down at them. Her fingers were curled around the iron spikes. There was no sensation in them. The nail of her left forefinger had broken. The broken piece was folded back on the nail itself. That was all, her hands gripping emptiness. The city below had vanished. The only thing she was conscious of was her own pain and Steven's. It was over, their brief delusion of happiness, of joy, of fulfillment, and completion.

She tried to speak, finally succeeded. She said slowly, "It wasn't in the cards, Steven. It wasn't meant to be that way. It was too good to be true."

She groped for stability, acceptance. Steven was married. His wife refused to release him. The choice had to be Sara's. Acceptance wouldn't come. Instead, flame swept through her, a burning. She clenched her teeth under the drive of a dreadful blind resentment, against herself and Steven for their initial blunder, the way they had wrecked their lives at the start, against Sara Hazard's clinging and the way the cards were stacked. She wanted to fight, to protest, to hurl defiance at the woman with the narrow white face and the sleek, golden head who held Steven in escrow, retarding and defeating him and making his existence meaningless, empty, a vacuum.

She wasn't aware that she spoke until she heard her own

voice with its forlorn attempt at steadiness.

"What did she say, Steve?"

Steven said in that same harsh monotone, "I put it up to her as soon as I left you this afternoon. I offered her practically everything. She refused. She laughed. She told me not only that she wouldn't give me a divorce, but that she was going to South America with me."

Cristie's grip on the iron railing tightened. "And you, Steven? Are you going through with it? Are you going away?"

"Yes."

His voice changed, thickened. He put his hand on her shoulder fumblingly. She shivered, didn't move as he continued, "There's nothing else to do. I've got to get away, Cristie. If I stay in New York and you're here—I wouldn't be able to stand it. No. Unless..."

Every instinct within Cristie cried out to her to complete that sentence, to throw Sara aside, treat her as though she didn't exist, fling her out of the way. The temptation was there, an almost overwhelming temptation. She couldn't do it. Something deep, elemental, held her back.

"No," she whispered. "No, Steve."

Steven's hand fell from her shoulder. He said quietly, "Then this is good-bye."

Good-bye! The night rocketed into a thousand pieces. Cristie was alone in the middle of a spinning darkness. Anguish shook her, immense, unbearable. She tried to call out. Her throat was sealed.

Steven's voice came to her dimly, from a long distance off. He was saying, "If it's got to be, Cristie, let it be fast." He went on talking. There was something about a ship, a ship that sailed on Monday. Monday—and this was Sat-

urday. All that Cristie knew was that Steven mustn't
leave her like this. He mustn't! She wrenched herself clear
of chaos, turned.

Steven was no longer there. He was crossing the terrace
with quick strides. He went through the glass doors. Had
he misinterpreted her silence? She had to see him again,
if only for a moment, to tell him the truth, tell him she
loved him and would always love him, no matter what
happened or how much distance separated them.

She started after him. The hall was crowded. She collided
with people. They kept getting in her way. She was forced
to a halt near the entrance to the dining room. Steven was
standing less than twenty feet away. He was talking to
someone. Who was it? Oh, Mary Dodd and Johnny.
Johnny left them. Steven looked dreadful. Mary Dodd's
face wore a frown of concern. He went on talking to her.
Mary Dodd looked frightened. She laid a hand on his arm,
interrupting him. Steven shook her hand off. He swung,
strode round a bank of azaleas and went into the living
room.

Was he looking for his wife? At the thought of them
together, weakness swam up around Cristie. She leaned
against the door frame.

Then she saw Steven again. He was going into Margot's
bedroom. He was only there for a moment, came out with
his hat in his hand. Had he left his hat in Margot's room?
Most of the men had put their things in the study. Cristie's
heart took a queer little sideways slip.

When she reached the spot where she had last seen him,
Steven was gone. The fear was there in her then, vague,
formless, unacknowledged. It steadied into deadly close-
pressing certainty when she paused beside the chair in the

recess beyond the bed on the far side of Margot's room and lifted Sara Hazard's cape of summer ermine. Again and again she sent her fingers exploring. She shook out the snowy folds. She looked on the seat of the chair, under the chair, on the gray felting, all around.

Steven had been in the room. He had no business there. Sara Hazard had dropped a gun into the pocket of her cape earlier that night. The gun was gone. And so was Steven.

Chapter Four
THROUGH THE RAILING

IT WAS A LITTLE after one when Steven Hazard left the St. Vrain penthouse. It was almost a quarter of two before Cristie went to the telephone.

She made herself face facts coldly. The square, black automatic that Sara Hazard had parked in her cape was no longer there. Steven was gone and Steven was in a dangerous frame of mind. His coolness, his detachment, his judgment had been scattered to the four winds by the events of the afternoon and evening. Anything might happen now. Anything. Cristie had to do something. The time for inaction was past. She had to locate Steven, get the pistol away from him and make him listen to reason.

Violence wasn't an answer to anything. The idea of it, and of what it would mean, was unthinkable. In spite of the dark shadow hanging over her, her clarity had returned. She saw things again in focus, objectively. She knew there was only one course to pursue.

Give Steven time to get home, if he was going home, and try there first. Don't think any further than that yet, one step at a time. It would take him anywhere from ten to twenty minutes to get to the apartment in Franklin Place. As long as Sara Hazard was in the penthouse there was no real cause for worry.

When she reached her bedroom the telephone was in use. A large, dark, masterful woman was talking endlessly to

someone named Mabel about a baby's bottle and a two
o'clock feeding. It was just before two when Cristie slipped
into the place the large, dark woman had vacated after
closing the door behind her. Cristie looked around, then
took the receiver off the hook.

She dialed the number of Steven's Franklin Place apartment. A voice answered. It wasn't Steven. It was the Hazard
maid, Eva Prentice.

Cristie said, "Is Mr. Hazard there? Has he arrived yet?"

And the maid answered, "No, Mr. Hazard isn't here.
Who is this calling? Is there any message?"

Cristie couldn't see the emotion evoked by the sound of
her round young voice, but a little stab of terror went
through her when the maid continued smoothly, "Would
this be Miss Lansing?" How did the woman know her
name? She had never been at the Franklin Place apartment. But Steven might have called her from there after
their first meeting. Cristie had an inkling then that the
Hazard maid, Eva Prentice, knew about herself and Steven.
She wasn't to realize until later how much the maid knew
about everything. She hung up without answering.

If Steven wasn't at the Franklin Place apartment, where
was he? She pushed the inertia of helplessness from her.
She couldn't go searching all over New York for him; to
intercept him was her only chance, to intercept him before
he and Sara met again. The point of interception had to
be the apartment on Franklin Place.

It was getting late. Sara Hazard would be returning there
in a short while. Steven would go back eventually. She had
to get hold of him first. The crowd was beginning to thin,
but there were still a lot of people milling around, laughing and talking and drinking and dancing.

She went back into her bedroom. No time to change now. She slipped into a black velvet evening coat with wide velvet sleeves, tied a black silk scarf over her head. Not the front door, she didn't want to attract attention. She left the penthouse by way of the side terrace and the service elevator.

The service entrance debouched on the pavement thirty feet from the front door of the apartment house. Cristie mounted a small flight of steps. Madison lay to the west, Park to the east. The street was dark, deserted. There were no cabs in sight.

.She was about to step out and start toward Park Avenue when she stood still. The doors of the main entrance were opening. A girl laughed, a man answered her. The couple descending the steps strolled away together.

Although the need for haste had become urgent, Cristie didn't move. Sara Hazard was descending the steps. Cristie recognized her instantly, her golden head was uncovered, shimmered palely above the long folds of the white ermine cape. Sara Hazard was also looking for a cab and had evidently reached the same decision as Cristie because she turned left, started to walk away.

She hadn't gone more than a few yards when she came to an abrupt halt. Cristie stared through the gloom. A man had stepped out of the shadows, a big man in a dark suit with a soft dark hat pulled down over her eyes. He stood directly in Sara Hazard's path so that she was automatically forced to a standstill.

Light from a street lamp shone down on the man's big shoulders, his rugged brow, on the outline of his jaw and chin. The man was Pat Somers, Assemblyman Clifford Somers's brother. Cristie was startled and a little bewildered. Cliff Somers had said that his brother Pat was in Albany with the Governor. Why was Pat Somers lurking outside Margot's penthouse? Because it was quite evident that he had been waiting there, and waiting for a purpose. He started to speak. Cristie couldn't help hearing him.

Pat Somers said, "Good evening, Mrs. Hazard. Don't run away." The words were even, unaccented. Their import wasn't.

Sara Hazard drew her cape tightly around her. Her voice had a nervous quality to it as she exclaimed, "Oh, Mr. Somers! But I thought you were out of town. At least— I don't know who—I mean, someone *said* you were. I thought ..." She stopped in the middle of a sentence.

Pat Somers reached out. He took Sara Hazard's shoulders in a huge tight grip. He said calmly, quietly, every word audible, "No. I'm not out of town. I'm right here. I was at home earlier this evening. I know what went on there. I saw you. Listen, Mrs. Hazard. This is a warning. Keep away from my brother Cliff. Stop your little game. I won't have it, do you understand, I won't have it. That's all. And I don't play ping-pong."

There was something singularly menacing in his trenchant tone. Sara Hazard jerked herself loose from the hands resting on her shoulders. She said vehemently, furiously, her silken ease torn to shreds, "You seem to think you own this town, Pat Somers. Well, you don't. And you can't bluff me. I can play tougher games than ping-pong myself."

Pat Somers reached out again. This time there was more than warning in his big, well-manicured fingers. His hands stopped in mid-air. They fell to his side. A man was running down the apartment house steps. His back was toward

Cristie. He called, "Oh, there you are, Mrs. Hazard. Gonna take you home. Damn shame pretty woman has to go home alone. Won't 'low it."

Cristie recognized the voice. It was Euen Firth and Euen seemed to be pretty well plastered. Sara Hazard welcomed Euen's arrival, tight or no tight. She took his proffered arm, said acidly, "Good night, Mr. Somers."

Euen's long cream-colored roadster was parked at the curb a little farther along. Euen helped Sara into it, got in himself. Pat Somers watched them drive away. The tip of his cigar glowed and ashed and glowed again. He took the cigar from his mouth, threw it in the gutter and, as the roadster disappeared around the corner, he started for the Avenue.

Cristie found a cab at the corner of Madison and Sixty-third. She gave the driver general directions. She dismissed the cab on the side street to the west, walked toward Franklin Place, paused near the opposite corner. Euen Firth's roadster was standing in front of Steven's apartment hotel, a big building overlooking the East River. Sara and Euen were seated in the cream-colored roadster. There was no sign of Steven up or down the block.

Perhaps he was in the rooms on the fourteenth floor already. Perhaps he had returned since she had called from the penthouse. But perhaps not. She must telephone again and make sure. She looked back along the dark side street. Yes, the garage was there, she had noticed it when she drove past. Its lights streamed out. Garages always had telephones. She turned her back on Franklin Place, walked toward it quickly.

The telephone was in a booth just inside the big doors. No one stopped her or interfered with her. Luckily she had change. She called the Hazard apartment. Again it was the maid who answered. Thank God. Steven *wasn't* home. She was in time. But she would have to hurry.

Back near the corner opposite the towering apartment house, dotted here and there with a few illuminated windows, she settled down to wait.

Sara Hazard was out of the cream-colored roadster. She was having trouble getting away from Euen. It was very quiet. Cristie heard Euen urging her to go down to Jimmy Kelly's with him for " 'nother little drink" but Sara refused. She said good-night curtly and disappeared through the big grilled iron doors.

The night was still warm but Cristie was shivering. Suppose Steven had gone in while she was telephoning from the garage? No, that was scarcely likely. If he had, Sara would probably have gone upstairs with him. Where was he and what was he doing? Pain seized her again, numbing her faculties, destroying her equilibrium. She climbed clear of it with effort, braced her shoulders against the brickwork of the wall against which she leaned in a dense bank of shadow and kept her eyes fastened on the apartment across the way and to the north.

Euen's car was still standing at the curb. He sat sprawled back against the cushions. Only the fact that he was smoking showed that he hadn't fallen asleep in an alcoholic stupor. A man and a woman entered the apartment hotel. A colored man came out and sloshed water on the steps, went in again. Someone was polishing the inside of the doors.

Fifty feet farther away a dim globe burned above the service entrance. When Cristie had been standing there for about ten minutes, a woman came out of it, a slender blonde in modish black. Euen Firth moved. He sat erect, put his hand on the door of the roadster. She heard him call, "Mrs. Hazard." The woman passed the main entrance, glanced at him curiously and continued on her way. Euen sank back. The woman wasn't Sara Hazard. The colored man was on the steps with another bucket of water. He spoke to the woman. Cristie didn't know that it was Eva Prentice, the Hazard maid. Presently Euen Firth drove away.

The apartment door opened. Cristie caught a glimpse of women on their knees with mops and pails. A clock somewhere struck three. The door started to close. It was Sara Hazard who came out. She had changed her evening gown for a dark suit and a small dark hat. Cristie caught the gleam of her hair beneath the hat brim. She was carrying her purse under her arm.

Where was she going at that hour of the night? There was a suggestion of watchfulness about her. Out on the Place, she paused, looking right and left.

A couple of stray cabs went past. An ambulance clanged distantly. The faraway murmur of traffic rose and fell. It was fainter now. New York was approaching its zero hour.

After that sharp right and left stare, Sara Hazard walked to the corner, the corner opposite the one on which Cristie stood well back in deep shadow. Sara Hazard turned into the side street running down to the river. A car was parked in the obscurity near the top of the short steep hill. Its back was toward Cristie. It was facing the East River Drive below. It was Steven's gray convertible.

Mrs. Hazard got in and switched on the lights. They did little more than make the darkness visible. There was no sign of Steven. Get as near as possible to the apartment,

Cristie thought, so as to catch him when he arrived.

The mouth of the steep side street was almost directly in front of her on the far side of Franklin Place. The car with Sara Hazard in it was some fifty feet from the corner. Cristie started across. The roadbed was smooth, even. She was in the middle of it when she jolted to a stop. There was movement in front of her, in and around the gray coupe.

Cristie's knee twisted under her and she almost fell. She recovered herself, stumbled over the curb, collided with a stanchion. She was oblivious, ducked around it and raced on, fighting for breath.

Less than thirty seconds later she stood motionless at the top of the hill. Her senses reeled crazily. The red tail light of the gray convertible, Steven's car with Sara Hazard at the wheel, was plunging down the precipitous grade and weaving from side to side.

A flash across the darkness beyond and below. The gray convertible hurtled out of the side street at a terrific rate of speed. It shot straight across the Drive, struck the iron railing on the far side, crumpled it like so much papier-mâché, sawed into the air, and dropped like a stone into the swirling waters of the black East River.

Chapter Five
FILE ON SARA HAZARD

GEORGE MORRIS, a paper salesman of Pelham, New York, was an eye witness of what took place. He gave the police an accurate account of it later. Morris was proceeding north along the East River Drive after a somewhat hilarious night at Barney Gallant's when the accident happened. Conscious that he was't in the best possible shape, Morris was driving slowly, a fact for which he was to thank his lucky stars forever after. Otherwise he would have been a gone goose.

The gray convertible with a woman in it cut directly across his path less than ten feet away. The crash, the leap into the air, the sickening dive, jarred every tooth in Morris's head.

He managed to bring his own car to a stop. He was shaking. Sweat covered him from head to foot. He wasn't the only one who raced for that jagged gap in the iron railing above the river. Running feet pounded the pavement, there were shouts, cries. They gathered volume. There! Where? The fence. God—look!

A few minutes earlier the Drive had been deserted. People began springing up out of the darkness. A policeman arrived. A radio car appeared. The crowd thickened. Someone must have telephoned because an ambulance pulled up in short order just after the police emergency squad rolled up and took over.

The throng of spectators, dense by this time, was ordered

44

back. A space was cleared. A wrecking truck eased its way to the broken fence above the river. Spotlights were trained on the sluggish black water. Two or three big policemen, stripping hastily, had already dived in. They were swimming around in circles and calling to each other.

The crane with chains suspended from it went down slowly. They had to try twice before the men in the water could dive down and fasten the chains securely round the car lying in the mud eighteen feet below. When it was almost up, the car slipped. A groan went up from the crowd. The whole process had to be repeated.

Pale light that was the precursor of dawn was coming up in the east when the hood of the submerged car at last broke the surface. Voices were raised. Someone moaned. The gray convertible belonging to Steven Hazard had gone into the river with a woman at the wheel. There was no woman in it now.

The car was empty.

Sara Hazard's gloves, her purse, her keys were in the tangled wreckage of the car that had been fished up out of the East River. Her body wasn't recovered for twenty-two days.

They were twenty-two days of unmitigated hell for Steven Hazard. Interviews with the police, with the searchers, with the detectives of the Missing Persons Bureau; it was the uncertainty that was the worst. August went by and September came and the days mounted into weeks. There was no news of any kind. Where Sara Hazard had been there was simply a void.

Steven Hazard's friends rallied around him, did what they could, Mary Dodd and Kit Blaketon, Pat Somers, his chief in the office and two or three others. He saw Cristie only once during that terrible interval. They met like strangers.

Steven showed no desire to be alone with Cristie. He was silent, remote, wrapped in a shroud of doubt and fear and torturing suspense. The South American trip was off. National Motors had sent another man to the Argentine.

For once anticipation of the dreadful ordeal that lay somewhere ahead lagged behind actuality when it finally came.

Sara Hazard's body was discovered floating in the waters off the North Beach airport by the boat patroling the seaplane lanes. It was taken to the morgue and subjected to extensive examination and various tests. Steven Hazard was summoned. The clothes had already been identified as the missing woman's, black silk suit, underwear with her monogram on it. Toeless sandals still clasped the once pretty feet, now shapeless and swollen. The hat was gone and the hair that had been bright gold was no longer bright. It was bleached and stained and bedraggled from long immersion in the shifting tides of the river.

The brown eyes were mercifully closed. But the body itself was a bloated and hideous caricature of the beautiful Sara Hazard. Not nice, not easy to take.

Steven Hazard looked at her under the watchful gaze of a group of officials. Assistant District Attorney Dorrens said, "You must allow for—certain differences. The—er—water, you know, and the length of time..."

Steven Hazard said, "Yes." The captain of the detective district raised an eyelid carefully. He indicated the clothing, the hair, what was left of the teeth, a bracelet embedded in the flesh. Hazard stood beside the drawer looking down. An iron rein held his emotion, his outraged sensibilities in check. He identified the body.

After a long moment he said huskily, "Yes. That's— my wife. That's—Sara." He turned away.

An autopsy was duly performed. Sara Hazard had been neither shot, strangled, poisoned nor stabbed. The lungs were full of water. She had been alive when she went into the river. She had been drowned as a result of the crash.

What had happened was clear. A late party, a projected excursion elsewhere. The Hazard convertible with the top down had been parked in its usual place when it wasn't in the garage, at the top of the sharply inclined street around the corner from the apartment hotel. Sara Hazard had lost control. The car had turned over when it hit the fence before diving into the river. She had fallen out, to be battered back and forth for all those days in the swiftly moving currents until her body turned up off the airport.

It was on the twenty-fifth of August that the fatal crash occurred. It was on September sixteenth that the body was found. Two days later Sara Hazard's body was buried in the little cemetery a couple of miles away from the Hazard farmhouse in lower Dutchess County. A cold September rain beat down on the handful of mourners. Cristie Lansing wasn't there. Mary Dodd and Kit Blaketon were, and Pat and Cliff Somers and Steven's chief.

That was on Wednesday. On the succeeding Monday, Steven Hazard returned to the office. Work was good for him, took him out of himself. His friends encouraged him. He began to look more normal. He went to the World's Series with Pat, spent an occasional evening at the Dodd house. Mary Dodd was very kind to him, very gentle. So was Kit Blaketon.

Steven was too much wrapped up in himself to notice the change in Kit or that Cliff Somers no longer dropped in at all hours. Mary didn't say anything. She talked of his work, of the future, made him talk.

Steven had closed the apartment on Franklin Place. He put the things in storage and moved to his club. He called Cristie once or twice, but it wasn't until after the first of October when a refreshing tingle of frost was turning the leaves, that he began seeing her regularly again. The first meeting was awkward, they were stiff and shy with each other.

The stiffness began to wear off. Steven would call Cristie from the office and they would meet for a quiet dinner and a play. They didn't do much talking. There were so many things that had to be left unsaid.

The shadow of Sara persisted. Cristie began to wonder with a dull ache at her heart what was going to happen and whether Steven would ever speak to her again as he had spoken that day in the little café around the corner from Margot's.

Late one afternoon in the middle of the month, Margot St. Vrain called Steven at his office and asked him to the penthouse for dinner and the evening. Steven thanked her, but said he had an engagement to dine with Mary Dodd and Kit Blaketon. Margot suggested that he bring the two women over after dinner. She said Harry Woods, the song writer, was going to be there, that he was going to try out a new number for them.

Steven spoke of Margot St. Vrain's invitation to Mary Dodd during dinner and Kit was enthusiastic about the idea. She hummed, "When the red red robin comes bob, bob, bobbin' along" with a touch of her old gayety and said, "Let's, Mary, I'd adore meeting Harry Woods. He's marvelous, absolutely grade A."

Mary was agreeable. While Kit was getting her hat, Mary told Steven she had been a little worried about the girl but didn't tell him why.

When they arrived at the penthouse, Margot received them cordially. Her fiancé, Euen Firth, her cousin Johnny St. Vrain and Harry Woods were there. Woods was a lean gaunt fellow with an attractive smile.

Steven introduced Mary and Kit. Woods resumed his place at the piano. Cristie came in during the middle of the new song. She slipped quietly into a chair near the door, a slim snow-white and rose-red figure in dark crimson wool that brought out the cherry-blossom texture of her skin, the dark cloudiness of her hair. She didn't single Steven out particularly, She gave him a smiling nod, accepted Kit Blaketon's sizing-up stare, returned Mary Dodd's pleasant half-smile and waved a hand to Johnny, leaning over the piano.

The song over, they all congratulated Woods. Euen Firth reappeared, followed by a colored maid wheeling a small bar. Drinks were served. Conversation became general.

As usual Euen helped himself to the liquid refreshment, his weak, good-natured face outfitted with a placating and permanent smile.

Cristie was waiting for a chance to talk to Steven, but to her annoyance Euen devoted himself to her. Her attention wandered. Toward what she hoped was the end of a long story about a Mexican and a goat, she glanced up. To her surprise, Euen wasn't looking at her; he was looking at Steven who was talking to Margot and Miss Dodd on the other side of the room. There was no vacuity in Euen. His eyes were owlish, intent. As she watched, his aimlessness returned. He put a hand on her shoulder and finished his tale, echoing Cristie's polite mirth with a cheerful guffaw.

Cristie was puzzled. It was no more than that, then. Another man and woman came in, and, later, Pat Somers arrived. He was accompanied by his brother Cliff. Cristie hadn't seen either of them since the night of the party. That was what she called it herself, the only thing she permitted herself to call it. She averted her mind swiftly, pulled down a shutter. The act was automatic. She was getting used to it. Pat greeted Margot and Johnny, turned to Mary Dodd. He seemed glad to see her.

"I called the house and they told me you'd be here," he said.

A look of understanding passed between them.

Kit Blaketon joined Johnny on the other side of Woods. The girl had been laughing and talking a moment before, red hair tossing vivid fire around the pretty, pointed face. It changed as Cliff Somers neared the piano. There was a beseeching air about him as he said, "Hello, Kit."

Kit Blaketon stared back at him stonily. "'Lo, Cliff."

It was the merest scrap of a greeting, indifferent, curt, uninterested. She turned back to the song writer, threw an arm around his shoulders.

"Go on, Harry," she urged, "don't stop playing."

Woods looked up at her with a grin. "All right, baby, what'll you have?"

Kit Blaketon's voice, clear, metallic, rode the room as she answered, "Play 'Get out of Town,' darling. That's the only tune I can think of at the moment."

Cristie watched the good-looking young politician flush and pale. How cruel girls could be when they wanted to! Then she stopped thinking about the curious incident.

Steven was crossing the room. Beside her he said in a low voice, "I want to talk to you, Cristie." He looked different. There was an air of purpose about him somehow.

She said, "My room, down the hall."

She was standing at one of the tall windows beyond her drawing board when Steven joined her. He paused just inside the door, his tall broad-shouldered figure, his dark head, outlined against the white paneling. He was thinner and older but the light was back in his face, the light Sara had almost succeeded in crushing out.

"Cristie!" His voice had a ring to it.

"Yes, Steven." Her own was none too steady, her own small dark head was lifted. She was shaking inwardly. "You—wanted me for something?"

Steven was holding a cigarette in his lean brown fingers. He ground it out in an ash tray. He said, "That's just it. Yes, Cristie. I *do* want you. It's time now. All the other is gone. It's finished, done with, over."

Cristie's hands were clasped in front of her. Her fingers tightened. The dark pool at the bottom of her mind stirred a little. Was anything ever over completely? Did the past ever really bury its dead? Or were they just tucked away conveniently out of sight? She turned to the window, looked out into the clear, star-spangled autumn night, said on an uneven breath, "Oh, Steven, Steven—I don't know. Can we ever ...?"

Steven was close to her. He put strong gentle hands on her shoulders, swung her round until she faced him. His eyes dove deeply into hers. She couldn't get away—realized, a thin glow of rapture beginning to pervade her, that she didn't want to.

Steven continued, his eyes holding hers, "Yes, Cristie. We can. We can and we will."

The core of darkness within her refused to dissipate, continued to send out creeping tentacles. "Are you sure, Steven?" she whispered.

Steven held her away. She looked at the dancing specks in his steel-bright eyes. The irises were ringed with black.

He said steadily, "Yes, Cristie, I'm sure. I let you go once. I'm not going to let you go again. Cristie, Cristie." His grip tightened. "Don't you understand? I love you. We have a right to each other. And by guess or by God, anyone who tries to stop us now—well, it's going to be just too bad. Cristie, tell me what I want to hear, tell me, darling, tell me!"

Cristie didn't answer at once. She was deeply moved. But that inner weight was difficult to throw off. Steven's hands fell from her shoulders. His eyes searched the small white face she lifted to his. Her lips parted. Her lashes opened wide and glory blossomed in the violet eyes set at a tilt under the delicate brows.

"Steven," she cried in a low radiant voice. "Oh, Steven, Steven."

Her arms were around his neck. He strained her to him. Their lips met and the room, the penthouse, the whole sorry world were left behind.

They clung passionately to that moment, a moment in which they were in another atmosphere beyond time and beyond space with only themselves and a thin strain of music that was Harry Woods in the distant living room playing, magically, *Begin the Beguine.*

> *To live it again is past all endeavor*
> *Except when the tune clutches my heart;*
> *Yet there we are, swearing to love forever,*
> *And promising never, never to part.*

Cristie withdrew her lips from Steven's, burrowed her forehead in the hollow of his shoulder. "Never, Steven," she murmured. "Never?"

Drawing her closer, Steven said, "Never, darling, never. Sara's gone. Don't worry about her any more. You mustn't. It isn't necessary. I know things about Sara that . . . Listen, sweet, on the night Sara died . . ."

Something warned Cristie. She realized afterward that it was the music. It had become imperceptibly louder. She raised her head. Steven had his back to the door. His bulk obscured her view. She twisted sideways, looked past him.

The door leading into the hall was settling noiselessly into its frame.

Someone standing outside in the corridor had opened and closed the door a moment earlier. Steven had been speaking of Sara and the night of Sara's death. . . . The fear was back in Cristie, a new fear that added itself to the other and thrust her down again into swirling eddies of uncertainty and terror.

That night Christopher McKee returned to New York from Rio de Janeiro. He was back at his desk in the Homicide Squad before morning. It wasn't until five o'clock on the following afternoon that he got the letter, a letter addressed to the Commissioner and sent up by messenger from Headquarters. The Inspector read it once and then again. He pressed the buzzer on his desk. When the door opened and Lieutenant Sheerer stuck in his head, McKee said without looking up from the sheet of paper he held in his hand:

"Get me the file on the drowning of Sara Hazard of 66 Franklin Place on August twenty-fifth."

Chapter Six
Post Mortem

THE LEAN, towering head of the Homicide Squad lounged back in the chair behind the desk near the single big window and studied the letter in front of him. The light gray of a well-cut, chalk-striped suit defined his muscular height, accentuated the deep tan of his clear olive skin, a tan produced by weeks of sun and sea. The cavernous brown eyes under thick dark brows, the powerful stern mouth that could unbend to humor were intent, speculative.

The letter read:

PoLIcE tAke NoTIce
SARA HAZARD 66 fRankLiN pLAce
did Not diE By accIDent. She was
MURDERED.

The Inspector turned the missive over, looked at the back, reversed it. The individual letters, in type, were pasted on narrow strips of yellow paper, which strips, in turn, were pasted on a sheet of white paper. The address on the envelope, *"Commissioner, Police Department, New York City,"* had been produced in the same way.

McKee ran the sensitive tips of his blunt fingers over the entire formation. Even without the accompanying memorandum, he would have been able to tell certain things. The letters themselves had been clipped from the packages of various brands of cigarettes. Paper and envelope were cheap and in widespread use; the paste was the ordinary commercial variety. He picked up the memorandum. No fingerprints. The communication had been posted at Grand Central.

In spite of the paucity of these details, the letter was informative. It was not the work of an entirely illiterate person. It was grammatical and there was a feeling for drama in it. The letters forming the name "Sara Hazard" and the word "murdered" were in large caps. The others were in various sizes of smaller type.

Tons of anonymous letters were recived both at Headquarters and his own Squad. They all got some sort of check. Ninety-five percent of them, perhaps more, was the product of disordered minds or of free-wheeling malice. The small remaining percentage really had something to offer. This one might belong to the latter category, it might belong to the former. The Scotsman didn't know. The only way to find out was to take a swing around the circuit, go over the ground thoroughly.

Lieutenant Sheerer brought the required papers and McKee read through the file, a hand shading his eyes. He assimilated the bare facts of Sara Hazard's death as a result of that downward crash into the river, checked through the report on the car. The brakes seemed to have been all right, but the steering gear, including the wheel, had been knocked to hell and gone. Nothing conclusive there. She might have lost control.

The hour of the fatal dive into the river detained him for a moment until he saw she had been out late at a party. He looked quickly at the Medical Examiner's report. Bruises, contusions, a broken shoulder, a smashed ankle, lungs filled with water—this last, unmistakable evidence of death by drowning. Body in water twenty-two days. He frowned, took the receiver off the hook, and called the Medical Examiner's office.

Fernandez, the Chief Medical Examiner, was still away on vacation. Petersen, the assistant who had done the autopsy, came on. In answer to McKee's question, Petersen said, after consulting the records:

"Yeah, Inspector, we opened the brain. She had a concussion, as well as those smashed limbs, probably got it when the car bashed through the fence. Some traces of alcohol. First degree—but no telling her susceptibility."

McKee said thanks, hung up and talked to Lieutenant Davidson, in command of detectives at the East Side precinct. Davidson had very little to offer. It had been the usual investigation. into death by accident. Nothing out of the way. Same old turaloo. Woman went to a party, got a little dizzy, decided to go in for more, and crashed up her car. Mrs. Hazard lived with her husband. No indications of homicide, nothing even to indicate it. When the body was found and identified, the case was closed.

Closed. McKee looked down at the letter on the desk. Perhaps. Peculiar word "perhaps," soft, easy spoken, putting off. It could create havoc. The Scotsman roused himself. Whatever else he was, he was a police officer first, last and all the time, and he used police methods. They were slow, laborious and plodding. They involved endless work, the accumulation of a vast body of fact from which the relevant details had to be selected and assembled. There were no miracles and he was no miracle worker. Successful results were achieved by the relentless pursuit of the last, the final scrap of evidence and the interpretation of its proper value.

Nothing to do now but get the whole picture clear. He rang for Sheerer and asked whether Todhunter was back from his vacation. Todhunter was. The little mousey man entered the inner office with a soft, sidling tread. No vacation could change the almost complete visual lack of personality of the detective who was one of the Scotsman's most valuable assistants. Hat, shoes, hair, face, clothing, were all approximately the same general tone, a grayish dun color. Todhunter was a man at whom no one would glance even once, let alone twice. It conferred a sort of cloak of invisibility on him. He could come and go as unnoticeably as a postman and without attracting any more attention.

The Inspector's sardonic, lined face relaxed. A pleasant smile curved his firm mouth, inclined to be uncompromising in repose. "Well, Todhunter," he said. "Have a good holiday?"

Todhunter beamed. "Swell, Inspector. Jumbo liked it too. We went up to the mountains. We had a great time.

Jumbo was Todhunter's obese and pampered mongrel with forty-two known strains in his pedigree. He was the detective's inseparable companion in his hours of ease and shared Todhunter's heart with the tall Inspector.

The little detective often wondered about his chief. The Scotsman never got tired. He seemed to have the strength of ten men. He could go days without rest or sleep. No problem was too big, or too small, for him to tackle. And he could fit into any niche, was equally at home at dinners and dances, on board yachts and at prize fights, as he was in Bowery smoke dives and Harlem gin shops.

McKee handed Todhunter the letter that had been sent up from Headquarters in the transparent holder. As the little detective glanced over its contents, the shadow of a frown creased his forehead. "Got the report on this case?" he asked.

The Inspector shoved the folder toward him. Todhunter looked up from a quick perusal of the first page. "I *thought* so," he said. "That's a funny thing, Inspector, I was on my way home from a plant on Bethune Street early that morning and ran into the crowd when they were hauling that car out of the river."

The Scotsman was surprised and pleased. His satisfaction dwindled as he listened to the little detective. Todhunter described the crowd, the confusion, and his own subsequent check which he had had made as a matter of course. It simply verified the present findings.

McKee glanced at the clock. It was a few minutes after five. "It's pretty late," he said. He gave a quick look at the file. "But we'll try him anyhow."

He dialed National Motors, got the engineering department and asked for Steven Hazard. A voice said that Mr. Hazard had gone for the day but he had left word that if anyone called, and he was expecting a call, he would be at George and Jean's on Forty-eighth Street.

McKee got up and reached for his hat. "Come on," he said.

As they went through the outer office, Lieutenant Sheerer stopped the little detective.

"Hold it, Todhunter. Dwyer wants you pronto to sign the statements in the Gainfort case. They're going to trial tomorrow."

Todhunter's face fell.

McKee said, "That's all right, go on down to the D. A.'s office. You know Dwyer. He's always talking about action.

Better give it to him. It won't take long. Join me at George and Jean's."

The cocktail lounge at George and Jean's was to the left of a small foyer. It was a smallish room with a dark oak floor, oak beams, scarlet table cloths, hunting prints on the paneled walls. It was fairly well filled. The head waiter bustled up.

McKee said, "I'm looking for a Mr. Hazard," on an interrogative note.

The head waiter bowed deferentially to the tall distinguished stranger. "Mr. Hazard? Come this way please. He's over there in the corner."

A tall man in his early thirties with a clever, sharply angled face was sitting alone, fingering a scotch and soda at the table the head waiter indicated. The Scotsman stared. He had seen Steven Hazard before. Where was it? Memory returned to him, the memory of that hot August afternoon just before he flew south. It was at El Capitan. There had been a girl with Hazard, the girl that Fernandez had said was one of the prettiest he had ever seen.

The Scotsman recalled her quite clearly. She had worn gray linen, had been first troubled and upset and then very happy.

Hazard was married to another woman at the time, a woman who had since died. By accident . . .

McKee wound his way through the tables, paused at the one at which Hazard sat. "Mr. Hazard?" he said pleasantly. "I'm Inspector McKee of the Homicide Squad."

Steven Hazard looked up. "Inspector McKee?"

His tone was surprised. It was also questioning. A shadow passed over his face. He said, "Sit down, Inspector. You wanted something?" There was a guarded air about him in spite of his ease, his casual motions, his smile.

"Thanks," the Inspector said pulling out a chair. "Yes. I wanted to see you about your wife's accident, the accident that resulted in her death on August twenty-fifth."

The shadow on Steven Hazard's face deepened. The line of his jaw sharpened. "But—" he threw out his hands —"I don't understand. I was over it all at the time with various members of the Police Department. Surely..."

McKee gestured apologetically. "I know how you feel, Mr. Hazard. But it's just one of those things. Red tape. It's got me in its toils too. These new rules and regulations are a nuisance. I've been away and under the new setup it's part of my job to turn in a personal report on all fatal accidents and suicides."

The Scotsman didn't know how well it went down. Hazard remained calm. His distaste, his brevity, were natural enough under the circumstances.

He told his story, what there was of it, in a direct, straightforward voice. It followed the main lines of what they already had.

The party from which Sara Hazard had gone to her death had been at Margot St. Vrain's. Again the scene at El Capitan flashed back to his mind. Was the girl in gray linen also at that party? If so, what had she done afterward? Look into it. He lit a cigarette.

"If I should want you later, out of business hours, to sign anything, you're living in Franklin Place?"

Hazard said no, he'd given up the apartment and had gone to live at his club. Mary Dodd, a friend of his and his wife's, had closed the place and put the things in storage. "It was too big for me," Hazard explained, "and besides..."

The Scotsman nodded his comprehension and tucked the name Mary Dodd away. "I can quite appreciate that, Mr. Hazard. And now, I trust you won't think I'm third-degreeing you when I repeat the routine question, where were you yourself on the night of your wife's accident?"

Steven Hazard spoke without hesitation. He said he had been at the St. Vrain party, had gotten bored, and had left before his wife. He wandered about a bit, dropped in at a couple of places for a few more drinks, and finally went home. Arriving there at, say, fourish, he had gone to bed. It was daylight before the police came to the apartment with the news of the accident.

Hazard said, "It wasn't until then that I knew anything about it."

After a few more questions concerning the car, the brakes, what kind of driver Sara Hazard was, McKee rose He thanked Hazard and started for the door.

Todhunter was standing in the archway leading to the foyer. The mousy little man was looking at the table the Scotsman had left. His gaze was riveted on the dead woman's husband. It wasn't until the Inspector joined him and they were in the lobby that Todhunter said in his soft accentless voice, "So that was Steven Hazard you were talking to in there, was it, Inspector? Poor guy. I must have been tough. He was standing there right in the crowd beside the river when they hoisted his car out and found it was empty."

The Scotsman's glance stood still abruptly on a bright, impossibly blue bird on the hat of an elderly woman talking to a waiter. He said, eyes narrow, ruminative, "Repeat that, will you, Todhunter?" And when the detective did, "You saw Steven Hazard there, when the car was

raised? That must have been at around half past five or
going on six. And Steven Hazard says he was at home
and in bed at four o'clock that morning and that he didn't
know anything about his wife's accident until the police
notified him later on."

Todhunter said, "I saw him there, Inspector, I don't
care what he says. I—" The little man stopped talking
suddenly. He laid a quick hand on McKee's arm. His
voice was the drift of a whisper. "Take a look at the dame
coming through the door."

McKee made a half turn. A dark-haired girl in a trim
tweed suit and a small brown hat was swinging across
the foyer. Her face glowed above a plaid scarf wound
round her white throat. As she passed them and went into
the cocktail lounge and started toward Steven Hazard's
table, Todhunter said in his low, mournful fashion, "Well,
I'll be jiggered. The trumps seem to be turning up. That
girl was there in the crowd that morning too. I mean
the night Mrs. Hazard was killed. She wasn't with Hazard. She was alone, standing some distance away. I noticed
her because she was in a white evening dress with a black
velvet coat thrown over it."

McKee didn't answer at once. He was still staring after
the girl with the remarkable eyes. A discreet inquiry of
the head waiter; the girl's name was Cristie Lansing, and
Cristie Lansing was the girl who had been with Steven
Hazard in El Capitan on the afternoon of the day before
Sara Hazard's death.

"Stay here and keep your eye on those two."

The Scotsman indicated the slim dark girl and Hazard,
heads close together in the cocktail lounge, and started
for the door.

Chapter Seven
A Dishonest Maid

THE LONG BLACK Cadillac was waiting in front of the restaurant. McKee got into it. He said to Miller at the wheel, "East," and reached for the two-way radio telephone in its cradle at the back of the front seat.

"Car CMK calling WNYF," he said into the receiver. "Car CMK calling WNYF." Back through the instrument came the voice of the First Department radio operator. "Go ahead, Car CMK." The Scotsman said, "This is Inspector McKee. Give me my office, Chelsea 3-7610." The voice came back again, "O.K. Stand by, Car CMK."

The two-way radio telephone was well worth the money McKee had invested in it out of his own personal funds. They couldn't get an appropriation for it. It was the same as the Mayor's. They still had to use the Fire Department station for two-way as the police weren't yet equipped. Traveling hurriedly from place to place in the city he had found it invaluable and except for a few dead spots under bridges or the el, it worked like a charm.

"Go ahead, Car CMK, here's your number."

That was the Fire Department radio operator. Lieutenant Sheerer came on. As the car crossed Lexington and headed for Third, the Scotsman said, "Sheerer? McKee. Send two men to relieve Todhunter as soon as he calls in, and tell him to get me through the car at once. I may be going to need men tonight. If there aren't enough on tap, get some. I'm going to sixty-six Franklin Place now. I'll get in touch with you later."

"O.K., Inspector." Sheerer's voice faded slightly as they passed under the elevated structure and sped toward Second. "Car CMK standing by," the Scotsman said. "WNYF standing by," the Fire Department radio operator said. McKee put the telephone back in its cradle.

He gave Miller directions. His first port of call was not the apartment hotel in which the Hazards had lived. It was the steep street around the corner that ran down sharply to the Drive and the river. Seated motionless in the back seat of the Cadillac on the spot in which Sara Hazard had been seated before that fatal plunge, McKee leaned back and lit a cigarette.

It was already dark. Conditions were much the same as they must have been on that August night except that there were more traffic and more people and it was colder. He absorbed the atmosphere, storing details for reference. Yes, it could be a bad spot for a woman with too much liquor aboard. The car could have gotten away from her.

Granting for the moment that it was accident, there were two rather startling discrepancies to be explained. One was the lie direct from Steven Hazard as to his presence on the scene when the wrecked car without anyone in it was raised. The second was the presence of the girl in whom Hazard seemed to be something more than interested.

McKee sat up. "All right, Miller," he said, "to sixty-six Franklin Place."

The vacated Hazard apartment had very little to offer. He interviewed the manager, the housekeeper, a couple of elevator boys, some cleaning women and a bath maid,

Laura Schmidt.

One of the elevator boys, Jerry Dorfman, and one of the cleaning women, Alice Fairfield, paired up in a tandem that gave the Scotsman pause. According to both of them, Sara Hazard gave not the slightest indication of being under the influence of alcohol when she left the apartment on the morning of her death.

The elevator boy had brought her downstairs shortly before 3 a.m. The cleaning woman had seen her go through the lobby. Of course you never could tell about some dames, Jerry Dorfman said, but she didn't look tight to him. And she didn't look tight to Alice Fairfield either and Alice Fairfield had seen her return home late and go out again plenty of times.

Both of them seemed to know what they were talking about. Its import was grave. Mrs. Hazard drunk was one thing, Mrs. Hazard sober was another, where an accident was in question. The Scotsman's mouth took a grim twist. If it was true, the precinct detectives had slipped up. They hadn't dug deep enough. The Scotsman proceeded to go on digging.

He found the bath maid, Laura Schmidt, at the dark end of a tunnel, literally and figuratively. She was down in the basement putting away her mops and cleaning powder and cloths and getting ready to go home for the day. Mrs. Schmidt added half a dozen new strokes to the picture that was beginning to take shape.

"Oh, she was a terror, that one," Laura said, referring to Sara Hazard, and smacked her lips over the telling of it. "I knew her maid Eva Prentice well and Eva said many a time what a shifty dame Mrs. H. was and what tricks she was up to. Eva was a smart one herself. She knew.

There wasn't much that went on in that apartment she didn't know. You ought to of seen the stuff that Mrs. Hazard had. Eva said it would of taken the crown jewels to keep her in clothes. Her bills! My! She bought tons of things and yet she was in debt over her ears. And then Eva said . . ."

Laura Schmidt paused in the middle of the flood of words, looked at the Scotsman. He smiled. "Yes, go on. Tell me what Eva Prentice said." Laura Schmidt was pleased. She resumed her narrative.

"Mrs. Hazard wanted to soak Eva a month's wages for an evening dress with coffee spilled on it that she'd never put on her back again. I said to Eva, I said, I wouldn't stay in a place where things weren't going right and I asked her why she didn't get another job. But she laughed and said Mr. Hazard always saw she got her money, and besides there were pickings. She wore Mrs. Hazard's size and Mrs. H. had such swell things. I often said to Eva I wonder why Mr. Hazard puts up with her and Eva said maybe he won't forever."

Laura Schmidt shook her head. "Why, the very night before she died, Mr. Hazard asked her for a divorce. You couldn't hardly blame him. Eva said to me they had a terrible fight. There was a big row about someone named Cristie, the girl that Eva heard Mr. Hazard telephoning to a few days before. Eva said to me she was surprised Mrs. Hazard didn't pull her gun on him."

The Scotsman put out a hand, halted the cleaning woman gently. "A gun, Mrs. Schmidt? Did you say a gun?"

Laura Schmidt nodded emphatically.

"Yes. A gun. Mrs. Hazard had a gun. Eva said to me, 'I saw it the other day when she was changing it from one bag to the other. You know,' Eva said, 'I'd never be surprised to pick up the paper and see she'd put a bullet through someone. Only the worst of it was,' she said, 'I believe she'd get away with it, unless there were twelve women on the jury. She ought to be hung,' Eva said. But I said, 'Eva take it easy, as the Irishman said hangin's too good for her, they ought to kick her tail.' And besides . . ."

McKee let the woman roll on. Laura Schmidt had plenty of information.

"This Eva Prentice," he asked presently, in one of her infrequent pauses. "What did she look like?"

"Oh, Eva was a good-looking girl," Mrs. Schmidt said. "She was young, around thirty, I guess, and she was blonde and had a good figure. Took care of it too, wouldn't eat much for fear of getting fat. She worried about her hips. Some people are like that. Now you take me . . ."

McKee didn't want to take the bath maid anywhere, but she was taking him plenty of places.

Mr. and Mrs. Steven Hazard didn't get along; he was in love with another woman; he had asked his wife for a divorce; she had refused to give him one and some nine hours later she had gone down the hill into the river in an accident.

Mrs. Schmidt's information was second-hand. Get hold of the maid. She had hated her employer. Hatred was a good tongue-loosener. The bath maid didn't know where Eva Prentice was. She herself had been off on the Sunday Mrs. Hazard died. There was a lot of excitement after that, police and detectives and reporters. She hadn't seen Eva again. And the apartment was closed.

The gun occupied the Scotsman. Sara Hazard's bag had been found in the wreck of the gray convertible. There was no gun in it. Nor had Sara Hazard been shot. Had she tried to turn that gun on someone else, and had that someone else retaliated? Those contusions, for instance, one or more of them might have been inflicted *before* the car plunged down the hill into the East River with Sara Hazard slumped unconscious at the wheel. Yes, that was the way it could have been. Nothing corroborative yet. But it began to add up.

Back in the lobby the Inspector asked for a telephone book, skimmed pages and found the name he wanted. In the Cadillac he gave Miller an address on East Seventy-third Street.

The loud-speaker erupted. "WNYF, calling Car CMK," McKee lifted the instrument from the cradle. It was Todhunter, relayed through the Fire Department. He had been relieved by two men from the squad. The girl and Steven Hazard were still at George and Jean's. McKee told Todhunter where to meet him, waited outside the well-kept old house on Seventy-third Street until the little detective arrived.

Mary Dodd received them in the long, softly lighted living room on the second floor. It was an attractive room, informal, gracious, the product of years and taste and culture. There was a portrait of the late Dr. Dodd over the fireplace. Miss Dodd put down her book and rose from her chair as an elderly maid ushered them in. She wore a crisp blue dress that matched the blue of her fine eyes.

"From the Police Department?" she said, looking from one man to the other. A frown puckered her forehead. She studied the Scotsman's lean tanned face.

McKee bowed. He introduced himself and Todhunter.

A shutter opened and closed at the back of Mary Dodd's

eyes when he said "Homicide Squad." Her lips tightened.
She said in a level tone, her brows raised, "Sit down, gen-
tlemen, will you please? What is it you want?" She was
pleasant and direct and at the same time she was worried.
There wasn't quite as much surprise in her as there had
been in Steven Hazard. Someone with incriminating
knowledge in his or her possession had sent that letter to
headquarters. Steven Hazard had spoken of this woman
as an intimate friend of both his own and his wife's. The
voice of conscience was not good enough. There was more
to the anonymous communication than that.

Mary Dodd seemed to be very fond of Steven Hazard,
but reticence entered into her when she spoke of the dead
woman whom she said she had known from a child. For
all her reticence McKee gathered that she hadn't cared
much for the late Sara.

She was a clever woman, wasn't deceived by his offer
of red tape as an excuse for reopening a case with *finis*
written after it. McKee felt around for something tangible
beneath the almost too pellucid surface of her unhesitat-
ing replies. Her championship of Steven Hazard was indirect but forceful. Sara Hazard had been headstrong,
rather difficult at times. Steven had borne her whims, her
extravagance, with admirable patience. They should have
had a child. It would have made Sara less self-centered,
more considerate.

The body recovered from the waters of the East River
had had very little to offer in the shape of information.
Nevertheless the late Sara Hazard was beginning to take
on life and substance. *Corpus delicti;* the chosen body.
Choose, select, single out, isolate from, for what? For
murder—as the anonymous letter charged? The ground-

work appeared to have been there. None of the people he had so far interviewed had given her a very good character.

He looked absently at the long-fingered white hands tapping a cigarette on a blue silk knee, touching the chair arm, smoothing the pages of an opened book, as he wandered at random over a variety of angles. Hands and voices were the most difficult to control. Miss Dodd was nervous. Her hands stood still when he mentioned the Hazard's maid, Eva Prentice. As early as that McKee got an inkling of Eva Prentice's importance.

Mary Dodd said, "I don't know what became of her or where she went. I never saw her again after Sara's death."

McKee pressed his advantage. "I'm going to be frank with you, Miss Dodd. We've been hearing things about that maid. She hated Mrs. Hazard. I'm very much interested in Eva Prentice."

Relief and a little thrill of fear went through the woman with the streak of white through her thick dark hair. Both of them were covered by an assumed indifference. "I'm afraid I can't help you much, Inspector."

McKee made a cast at random. "Come, Miss Dodd, you closed Steven Hazard's apartment for him after his wife was buried. You packed the dead woman's belongings."

Mary Dodd bit. She said swiftly, "Granting that the woman *was* a thief what was I to do? Steven was in no condition to be worried about a few trinkets and a fur coat. I did ask him to look over things, but, in the first place, he didn't know what Sara had and in the second, he didn't want to be bothered. You could scarcely blame him."

McKee went on asking questions. "That night at the party at Miss St. Vrain's, did you notice anything unusual that might have ... ?"

Mary Dodd shook her head slowly. "No. I can't say I did. It was a big party, of course. But I couldn't say that there was anything out of the way."

She could give him nothing like a complete list of the guests. Cristie Lansing's was among the names she mentioned. The Scotsman concealed his interest. Check on Miss Lansing elsewhere.

"Was Mrs. Hazard there when you left, Miss Dodd?"

"Yes, she was still there in all her glory and still going strong." There was unmistakable acridity in her reference to her dead friend.

"What time did you leave, Miss Dodd?"

"Not terribly late, a little after one. Kit ..."

"Kit?"

"Yes, my niece, Kit Blaketon, who lives with me, had left earlier and there was nothing to keep me."

Her inflection was too casual. "Was your niece at home here when you arrived?"

Mary Dodd said, "Oh, yes. Kit was in bed."

The Scotsman looked absently at a painting of the late Dr. Dodd in academic robes over the mantel. The anonymous letter calling Sara Hazard's death murder was a constant you couldn't get away from. You could do a number of simple examples with it. There was Eva Prentice, for instance. A thieving maid, a condoning employer; Hazard didn't look like an easy mark. He had ignored the theft of an expensive fur coat and half a dozen other articles including a wrist watch, a valuable compact and an emerald bracelet. Because the maid had something on him? Eva knew a good deal about her former mistress. Had she offered Hazard her information at a price? If so, and he had turned the offer down, the letter crying murder might be Eva Prentice's come-back.

Excellent as theory, worthless as proof—get after the woman, pick her up. She wasn't the only disturbing element at the root of Mary Dodd's very real perturbation. The attractive, cultured, sophisticated daughter of the late Dr. Dodd, eminent psychologist, was running around in mental circles beneath that calm exterior.

McKee got a line on her inner distress some five minutes later when they were leaving the house. They had said good-bye to Mary Dodd and were in the lower hall when the door opened and a girl came in. She was tall and reed-slender with flaming red hair and bright green eyes under a green beret.

There was a sullen tautness to her young face. She glanced at McKee and Todhunter without interest as though they were gas or electric men, said to the elderly maid waiting to show them out, "I'm starving, Eliza. I hope dinner's ready," and ran lightly up the stairs.

It was the glance the maid sent after her before turning to the police that was the tip-off. McKee's unreadable gesture to Todhunter said, "This woman knows something about that girl that she doesn't want us to know. Go to work on her." As the little detective laid a detaining hand on the maid's arm, McKee said aloud, "Must have dropped my fountain pen," remounted the stairs and proceeded noiselessly to the closed door of the living room.

- Pay dirt. The real McCoy with feathers on it. He could not see Mary Dodd, but he could hear her voice and its urgency; its pleading force told him plenty. Mary Dodd was saying, "—no matter how you feel about Sara and Clifford, Kit, don't mention it to anyone, *ever*. Particu-

larly to the police. You didn't see Sara go there the night
of Margot St. Vrain's party. You didn't go there yourself.
When you left the penthouse you came straight home.
You know of no connection whatever between Sara and
Cliff. The idea is *absurd,* impossible. Do you understand,
Kit?"

There was a pause. Then the older woman said in a
frightened tone, "Kit, Kit, what is it? Here, sit down.
Lean back. I'll get a pillow for your head. Don't move,
stay where you are . . ."

McKee was gone as sleekly and silently as a big gray cat
when Mary Dodd pulled open the door and ran out into
the upper hall. At the foot of the stairs he looked around.
Todhunter was nowhere in sight. A bell pealed distantly.
McKee let himself out. Presently the mousy little detective joined him on the pavement.

He hadn't gotten much. The maid, Eliza Welkie, had
been with the Dodds for some nine years. She didn't want
to give. Kit Blaketon had been living with her aunt since
Dr. Dodd's death. Miss Dodd was very fond of her niece.
The girl was engaged to a man named Clifford Somers.

It was at that point that McKee interrupted him. He
said swiftly, "Clifford Somers, Assemblyman Clifford
Somers. Pat Somers's brother."

Todhunter's mild eyes opened. He gave a small cough,
dusted his sleeve.

The Scotsman's nod was brief. He repeated Mary Dodd's
caution to her niece. "Cliff Somers and Sara Hazard . . ."
he said thoughtfully. "Yes. The going may get tough. I
don't know. We'll have to see."

Todhunter looked sideways at him. The match McKee
held to the tip of his cigarette was repeated in his eyes,

eyes that were bright and hard and fixed and unfathom-
able, in the shadow of the soft gray Homburg as he got
into the Cadillac.

McKEE stopped at a drugstore three blocks to the west. Not the radio phone this time, too many people listened in on the short-wave radio bands. He called the office, ordered tails on Mary Dodd, Kit Blaketon and Assemblyman Somers. When he told Sheerer he wanted to know where Pat Somers was and what he was doing, the lieutenant was startled.

"Yes, Pat Somers," McKee said drily. "The reopening of the case may put these people in motion. I want reports fast. Get me through the car as soon as anything comes in."

There was a restaurant in the middle of the block. The Scotsman hadn't eaten since morning. He sent sandwiches and coffee out to Miller, watching the radio, ordered a brace of chops and a tall glass of ale for himself.

His gaze roamed absently over the long, crowded room. A sense of haste and of the necessity for action possessed him. The anonymous letter and his subsequent procedure had stirred up the depths that lay beneath the surface of Sara Hazard's death by misadventure. His appearance on the scene had already produced some queer reactions. If there was anything really wrong he would have to move swiftly to prevent the destruction of such clues as might still remain.

To his alert faculties, the pod of Sara Hazard's death was overripe. At the first touch, it had sent out a cloud of feathery seeds, seeds that had in them dark implications and the threat of a new and evil flowering.

Devious paths were opening up, decidedly. He put down the glass of ale. Miller was at his elbow, saying, "The telegraph bureau wants you to call on the outside wire, Inspector."

The Scotsman entered a booth near the cashier's desk. Acting Captain Conley answered his ring. As McKee listened, his eyes began to shine.

The delegates were assembling. Miss Dodd and her niece, Kit Blaketon, had gone to Pat Somers's home on East Eighty-first Street. Clifford Somers had turned up there after several speeches in the district. Pat himself had arrived a few minutes later. Steven Hazard and Cristie Lansing were on their way down from Ben Riley's to join the gathering. The tailing detective had heard Hazard give the cab driver Pat Somers's address.

Pat, the strong man. McKee got what it meant. These people were all frightened. They were beginning to move. They were going to Pat for advice, counsel, perhaps an attempt at a fix, perhaps to get him to tell them how to play it. They all held cards, that seemed now a certainty. What those cards were it was up to him to discover.

He paid his check and left the restaurant. Todhunter met him on the street near the politician's high-stooped brownstone house crushed between two apartments. He saw several of his other men stationed unobtrusively up and down the block. Accompanied by Todhunter, he mounted the steps and rang the bell. A grim-visaged elderly woman in a violent, plaid, silk dress opened the door. The Scotsman asked for Pat Somers.

The woman said, "I don't know. If you'll wait here,

I'll see."

McKee didn't wait. He was just behind the woman as she went along the hall and opened the door of Pat Somers's office. The Scotsman got a quick glimpse of the room and its occupants. Pat was seated behind the desk at the far side, big, solid and quiet. Mary Dodd and her niece, Kit, were in chairs to the left of the desk. Pat's brother and Kit's fiancé, Assemblyman Somers, stood leaning against the ornate and hideous marble mantelpiece on Pat's right. There was an air of arrested tension at the elderly woman's entrance.

Pat looked up at her. "Yes, Julia," he said.

The woman responded with a jerk of her thumb hall-ward and a whisper in Pat's ear. Somers pushed back his chair and rose. He strode heavily across the worn rug. The others stared, even Cliff Somers. His gaze, fastened moodily on the brass fender in front of the empty grate, lifted. He followed his brother with his eyes.

McKee stepped over the threshold.

Pat Somers pulled erect with a jerk. Hot blood rushed into Pat's face. His eyes were blue ice under scowling brows. Looking fixedly at the Scotsman he said in a cas-ual voice, "Get the hell out of here, McKee. You've got no business here. This is my house. Get out!"

The Scotsman returned his gaze measure for measure. He said suavely, "I am fully aware of your rights, Mr. Somers, and you know me well enough to be sure that I am also aware of the rights of a police officer in pursuit of his duty." McKee's eyes continued to hold Pat's.

Somers scowled. "Duty, hell. Out, McKee. Your duties don't include this kind of thing."

The Scotsman shook his head. "That's where you're

wrong." His cavernous brown gaze left the big man in front of him, traveled slowly around the room as he said, "I'm here on business. That business is an investigation into murder."

"Murder!"

The word came from Pat. It was backed up by the same shocked inquiry in the three white faces behind him. The small comfortable study was very still.

"Yes," McKee answered steadily, "the murder, what I believe to have been the murder, of Sara Hazard in the early hours of the morning of August twenty-fifth."

He turned. Steven Hazard and Cristie Lansing had entered the house while he was talking. They had heard what he said. They stood, side by side, not ten feet away, immobile, frozen, the breath stopped in their throats. Steven Hazard made a strangled sound that was between a cry and an oath. His lips clamped themselves tightly together. Cristie Lansing's white lids fell. She swayed.

McKee said with salutary sharpness, "Come in, Mr. Hazard. You're just in time. You too, Miss Lansing. We've all got to have a little talk."

That brought the girl back. McKee held the door open, waved them ahead of him into the room. Pat Somers exchanged a look with Steven. There was warning in it. He pulled out a chair for Cristie, resumed his own seat behind the desk. Mary Dodd waved to the new arrivals. There was pain in her tightly compressed lips as she looked at Steven. The vibrant, red-haired Kit Blaketon kept on staring at the floor and Cliff Somers continued to devote his attention to the minarets of the gleaming brass fender.

McKee remained standing. They all waited. A black cat

strolled out from behind Pat's desk, yawned widely, and extended itself full length in the middle of the worn rug.

About to speak, McKee paused. There was a rap on the closed door. It opened and Captain Pierson entered the room. Pierson advanced to the Scotsman and delivered a whispered message. McKee nodded. He turned to Clifford Somers.

"Assemblyman," he said, "I'd like to talk to you alone in another room."

The young man looked at him. His face sharpened, hardened. He didn't say anything; followed McKee out of the office without a word. There was no response from any of the others. *Sit tight* was the general attitude. They were sitting very tight indeed.

McKee paused for a word to Pierson and Todhunter in the hall. Pierson entered the office the Scotsman had vacated. Todhunter moved toward the front of the house and the Inspector went, behind Clifford Somers, into a big, old-fashioned, gloomy parlor on the far side of the house.

The Scotsman took out a cigarette and looked over it at Somers. He said, "There's no use my wasting your time, Assemblyman, or letting you waste mine. What, exactly, were your relations with the late Sara Hazard?"

There was a belligerent scowl on Clifford Somers's handsome, boyish face. He stared the Scotsman full in the eye, thrust his hands into the pockets of his gray sack suit and said, "None."

McKee recognized the qualities that had enabled Pat to make his young brother a success in his district. Cliff Somers had daring, courage, a good presence and a capacity for lying convincingly. Without the knowledge that had just been imparted to him by Pierson, he might have been deceived by the trenchant brevity of the young man's reply.

"That won't do, Mr. Somers. In the first place, it isn't true." His tone changed. There was a ring to it as he continued swiftly, "What were you doing in the neighborhood of the East River Drive and Franklin Place in the early hours of the morning on which Sara Hazard went through the fence into the river?"

The young Assemblyman's jaw thrust itself forward. "Nuts and double nuts," he replied calmly.

"Nevertheless you *were* there." McKee was affable. "Patrolman Kenney saw you there and spoke to you."

Somers couldn't control his color. Pallor circled lips he managed to hold steady as he said, "All right. So what? This is campaign time. I represent this district. I was at a meeting at the Penobscott Club, dropped into the St. Vrain's party for a while, met some of the fellows later and had a few drinks. I started home, saw the crowd and stopped to see what it was all about. What's wrong with that?"

McKee said, "I think you'd better sit down. There are a number of other questions I want to ask you."

Clifford Somers didn't sit down. He paced the floor while the Scotsman went on with that exhaustive examination in the big gloomy parlor.

In the office on the other side of the hall, Pierson crossed and recrossed his solid knees under the covert scrutiny of the people seated there in silence. Pat Somers's cool blue gaze cupped and steadied the men and women around him in a rough semicircle.

Cigarette smoke, an occasional murmur from one to

the other. At the end of three or four minutes, Pat rose
from behind his desk and walked to the door. Pierson
let him go. He had his orders. In the little room next to the
office, Todhunter slipped quietly behind one of the heavy
velvet curtains as Pat Somers came in.

He watched the big man through a chink in the folds
of a faintly dusty maroon velvet. Pat Somers closed the
door softly behind him. He crossed to a safe in a corner,
knelt down and twirled the dial. The door of the safe
swung open. Pat reached in and took out something
wrapped in brown paper. He laid the parcel on top of
the safe, ripped off the paper, crumpled it up and threw
it into a trash basket. His back was turned and the little
detective couldn't see what it was that he had removed
from the safe.

Todhunter wanted to see. The room was very still. The
slightest sound would put Pat Somers on his guard. Todhunter edged forward, bringing the curtains with him.
Pat was taking a penknife out of his pocket. He shot open
the blade.

Todhunter put the curtains behind him and moved
noiselessly across the floor until he was directly in back
of Pat Somers. He took a quick step sideways and his
hand flashed out.

Pat Somers was big, bulky and powerful, Todhunter
was a mere wisp of a man. When necessity required it, the
little detective could move like lightning. That was what
he did then, fading across to the door, through it and into
the hall. He made a bee line for the parlor before Pat Somers really understood what had happened.

Ten minutes later McKee re-entered Pat's office. He had
dismissed Clifford as soon as Todhunter appeared. The

;cotsman was followed by the mousy little detective carry-
ng a square black box. "Plug it there," McKee ordered,
)ointing to an outlet. Todhunter laid the box tenderly on
he floor and obeyed.

McKee nodded his satisfaction, turned his survey on the
;tiffness of the motionless watchers. Anger, astonishment,
:uriosity, suspense in that loosely assorted group. No one
;poke.

McKee stood erect. His glance touched each one of them
in turn. He told them about the anonymous letter. He
swung on Steven Hazard. "You lied to me, Mr. Hazard,
about your presence on the scene at the time of your wife's
death. You *were* there. So were you, Miss Lansing. So," he
shifted to Clifford Somers, "were you, Assemblyman." His
gaze rested on Mary Dodd. "You cautioned your niece," he
indicated Kit Blaketon, stiff white face framed in the flaming hair, "to keep evidence from the police." He looked at
Pat Somers, smoking a cigarette in short quick puffs. "A
few minutes ago Mr. Somers, *you* deliberately tried to destroy evidence, vital evidence concerning the killing of
Sara Hazard."

He went on with a tired certainty more compelling than
any threat. "Sara Hazard was murdered. The details of
exactly how it was done are not yet clear but there was a
motive for her murder. I am now going to show you a
motive, a motive that could have influenced everybody in
this room. Sara Hazard came to this house and paid Clifford
Somers a visit on the night of the St. Vrain party. From
what I have been able to gather, she left the party after
telephoning to Clifford Somers at the Penobscott Club to
meet her here, returning to the St. Vrains' afterward."

The Scotsman didn't address any of them personally,

spoke as though he were instructing a jury.

"Kit Blaketon followed Mrs. Hazard here from the St Vrains', saw her enter this house. Sara Hazard had a conversation with Clifford Somers that night. Kit Blaketon was probably outside and couldn't hear it, but Pat Somers could. Pat Somers had come home unexpectedly from Albany.

"Pat listened to the conversation between his brother and the dead woman. He not only listened to it, he made a record of it on a machine he kept handy in the next room, which is connected with this by a hearing and a recording device. Quite natural for him to have such an arrangement and such a machine. When you're in politics you have to make sure bargains are kept. Gratitude so often transforms itself into a welch. Well, Pat Somers was in the other room when he heard his brother and Sara Hazard talking. He turned on the recording device. That record I am now going to play for you."

There was a moment of stricken silence. McKee turned to Todhunter. He nodded. The little detective pushed a lever on the black box. The silence fled. It was broken by the faint scratching whirr of the needle as the record that Pat Somers had tried to destroy a few minutes earlier began to go round.

Chapter Nine
For All to Hear

"Yes, Mr. Somers. It was *very* interesting."

Sara Hazard's recorded voice was audible in every corner of the room.

To more than one of those people, wooden dolls in an arc, the vision of Sara Hazard herself, as she had been on that distant August night, recreated itself in detail, the black and gold of an expertly executed evening gown following the lines of her long slim body, the curve of her breast, golden hair curling away from the narrow, chiseled face. The record continued to revolve, gave out the creak of a man settling back in his chair. Clifford Somers's voice came from the machine.

"All right, baby. Go on with your story. I always did like fairy tales."

Sara Hazard's recorded tones were liquid honey. "Does the name Dr. Karl Dennison mean anything to you?"

From Clifford Somers, "If it does, what about Dennison?" The demand was rough.

Sara Hazard: "Nothing, nothing, except that I happen to know Dr. Dennison rather well. One night he got drunk, got maudlin, started confessing. He knew the woman's husband, you see. That's why he felt so badly about it. You know the woman I mean?"

The whirring needle filled a pause. Sara Hazard's voice continued, bearing down. "The woman I mean is, or rather was, Mrs. Trembath, Claire Trembath. Too bad she had to die so suddenly after that rather strange operation. Before it was performed she told the doctor all about the very uncomfortable situation in which she found herself. The man who was responsible, and it wasn't her husband, had a good deal to answer for."

The Scotsman watched Cliff Somers, seated beside his brother. His head was bent. The room was cool. Perspiration stood out on the younger man's forehead, rolled unchecked down cheeks that were drawn, colorless.

The synchronization of his present posture with the reply coming out of the amplifier was striking. His recorded voice was a mutter:

"I was a kid. I didn't know what I was doing. I didn't know it was going to turn out that way."

Sara Hazard's answer was gently commiserating. Her living voice had been stilled forever but it reached forward out of the past and struck again, vibrant with threat: "It wouldn't be *very* nice, would it, Mr. Assemblyman Somers, if this particular incident in your amorous past should become public property? After all, as an accessory before the fact, it is a crime, you know; you would be liable. They mightn't prosecute you, but if the District Attorney went after the doctor, your appearance on the witness stand would be a big help to you in the coming campaign, wouldn't it?"

The coming campaign. The Scotsman's eyes were grim. The campaign that was now on. The needle continued relentlessly to travel round. There were sounds as well as voices. There was the sound of a chair being pushed back as though Clifford Somers had jumped to his feet. "You blackmailing...." The voice on the record broke.

Sara Hazard interrupted him coolly. "You hit the nail right on the head. I want money. I want a thousand dollars to start with, and I want the thousand tomorrow."

Clifford Somers, after another pause: "All right, baby, you've got me behind the eight ball. But where the hell would I get that kind of dough on such short notice?"

Sara Hazard said, "Pat's got plenty, hasn't he?"

McKee's gaze shifted to Pat Somers. His face, the thoughts going on behind it, were unreadable. But he was suffering. So was Kit Blaketon. She looked like a reproduction of herself in papier-mâché, a distorted and lifeless reproduction.

On the record the dead woman continued: "Pat trusts you. He won't suspect anything. You can give him some song and dance. I realize you wouldn't want Pat to know that his beloved younger brother, the rising politician, has gotten himself in such an unsavory mess."

It was tough to take. Clifford Somers flushed darkly. He stared steadily at the floor. This time his demeanor contrasted with the reply coming from the amplifier: "O.K., lady. I'll see what I can do. But you're playing a dangerous game and you'd better *watch your step.*"

A scornful little laugh from Sara Hazard. "I love danger. But I'm going to tell *you* something. You try to double-cross me and you'll get yourself into a real jam. You understand? I want that thousand tomorrow, not later than six o'clock."

Another whirring lull. Clifford Somers's response on that August night must have been a nod because Sara Hazard said, "All right. See you later."

There was the sound of a door closing. That was all. Todhunter pushed the lever. The whirling disk came to a stop.

The stillness was profound. It was dissipated by Pat. Pat

took out his handkerchief and sneezed into it resoundingly. At the small homely noise they all stirred. Cliff Somers sat up slowly. His muscles relaxed. Something like sanity returned to his eyes. He made an effort to swallow. Sinewy fingers loosened the collar at his throat.

The others continued to sit as they were. Cristie Lansing was huddled down in her chair. Her eyes under the delicate black brows were cloudy with distaste and some other and more baffling emotion. Steven Hazard's long jaw had a bitter brooding slant to it. The tell-tale vein in his temple had thickened. His dead wife had been made to speak again and to brand herself publicly out of her own mouth as the blackmailer she was.

Kit Blaketon's pointed face framed in elfin red had a crumpled look as though she were trying to rouse herself from sleep, as she moved the green eyes from a steel engraving on the opposite wall to the man to whom she was engaged and from whom she had been estranged.

It was Mary Dodd who spoke, her dark head with its plume of white lifted. She didn't seem to be addressing anyone in the room as she said, nausea and exhaustion freighting her voice, "It was all so unnecessary. We..."

Pat Somers didn't let her complete the sentence. He did erupt then. He cut Mary Dodd short with a deep, savage "So that's that, McKee. And now what do you propose to do about it?"

There were a number of things the Scotsman intended to do. He didn't intend to tell Pat Somers what they were. He took testimony briskly from all of them, individually and together as to where they had been and what they had done on the night of August 24th and the early morning of the 25th.

It was almost midnight when he left the house. He returned to the office where he made the necessary arrangements for corroboration and checking, with independent evidence if possible, the various tales that had been told.

At half past eleven the next morning Commissioner Carey called him. The Commissioner wanted to see him. The thin, dark, distinguished head of the New York Police was unsmiling when he greeted McKee in the paneled room on the second floor of the long gray building on Center Street at two o'clock that afternoon. There was no foliage in the vicinity to mark the season, but a brilliant autumn sky arched itself over the Police Academy across the way.

McKee dropped into a chair in front of the Commissioner's desk.

Carey said at once, "This about Pat Somers and his brother is bad business, Inspector."

McKee understood what lay behind Carey's summons, his careful utterance, knew the pressure that must have been brought to bear, indirect, but none the less formidable. The brakes had probably been applied in the usual way. He could almost hear a powerful and nameless emissary saying to Carey, "Look here Commissioner, you'd better tell that fellow McKee to watch what he's doing. Pat Somers is no slouch in this town and neither is his brother. It's ridiculous to think of Pat conniving at murder. The police have nothing on him. Any kid could get into a scrape. That's all there is to it."

The Scotsman lit a cigarette. "I'm glad you did send for me, Commissioner. If you hadn't, I would have come to you myself."

He described Sara Hazard's death, sketched the outlines of what he felt sure was murder made to look like accident on the previous August 25th. He described his own movements after receiving the anonymous letter and the incriminating material he had unearthed.

He enumerated the suspects, gave their possible motives. Sara Hazard was blackmailing Clifford Somers. She had plenty on him and he had more than sufficient reason for putting her out of the way. The same thing went for Pat. Pat was wrapped up in that young brother of his. He knew exactly what Sara Hazard was doing, knew that it would mean the ruin of his brother's whole political future, or else continued bleeding, perhaps for years.

"Why on earth," the Commissioner asked in a troubled voice, "did Pat Somers keep that damned record?"

The Scotsman stroked a silk-clad ankle. "It's simple, Commissioner. We rise and shine. Pat wanted Clifford to go up in the world when he married. Cliff was engaged to that red-haired niece of Miss Dodd's. They're folks. There's no doubt that the girl herself was insanely jealous of Sara Hazard, followed Sara Hazard from the St. Vrain party to the Somers house on Eighty-first Street, was outside watching when Sara Hazard left. Pat Somers kept the record because at the proper time he wanted to be able to give Kit Blaketon definite and conclusive assurance, if it became necessary, that there was no emotional entanglement between Sara Hazard and young Somers."

Carey interrupted him.

"I get it," he said.

"Then there's Mary Dodd," McKee continued. "She's very fond of the girl. Her own romance ended in tragedy; she didn't want her niece's prospective marriage broken up—and she knew it was seriously threatened. She'd borne with Sara Hazard for a long while, knew in general terms the sort of woman she was. Her sympathies lay with the husband, Steven, who's a close friend of hers. Mary Dodd is a clever, intelligent, decisive woman. I don't think she'd hesitate for a moment to commit murder if she decided that it was necessary."

Carey glanced at reports on his desk. "Both Miss Dodd and the niece were at home according to these."

McKee said thinly, "Turn about is fair play. They can alibi each other."

"Servants?"

"The two maids slept at the top of the house."

McKee moved on to Steven Hazard and Cristie Lansing, described the scene in El Capitan.

Carey said frowning, "How did the girl get over to that river bank? What did she say? You talked to her at Pat Somers's last night, didn't you?"

McKee shrugged. "She told me what was obviously a cock-and-bull story. She took a walk."

"You let her get away with it?"

"I let her think she did. That girl knows a lot. I'm going to let her roam on a loose rein, a very loose rein. Because I have a notion that sooner or later she'll lead us to where we want to get. She's in love with Steven Hazard and Hazard's in love with her. He asked his wife to give him a divorce. She refused, declared she was going to South America with Hazard, who had been offered and had accepted a post there. Pat knew this, Cliff knew it. In fact they all knew it.

"That's a point I want to insist on. Once removed from their combined sphere she could have carried on her blackmail without the threat of bodily harm. As for Hazard, he would have been saddled, alone and in another country, with a woman whom he hated and despised. Well. Sara Hazard didn't go to South America. She went down the hill into the East River. There you have it. There's only this to add. We have rock-bottom, cast-iron evidence against Cliff Somers and by implication against his brother Pat as far as motive goes. What, under the circumstances," the Scotsman leaned forward and his brown eyes met the Commissioner's gray ones, "do you expect me to do?"

Carey sat silent for a while. Then he nodded reluctantly. "You know I respect your judgment, McKee. I just wanted to be sure. Did young Somers say whether he paid when the woman put the heat on him?"

The Scotsman's smile was not humorous. "Clifford Somers said nothing. Pat told him not to talk; told me that if I wanted to question the boy further I'd have to put him under arrest. Of course"—the Scotsman gestured—"clever fellow, he knows that I haven't got a case for the D.A.'s office yet."

The Police Commissioner sighed. "I talked to Pat a little while ago. He had to agree when I insisted that he send Cliff Somers down. Cliff's outside in the other room now. Let's have him in and we'll ask him about the money."

He rang the buzzer and Clifford Somers was ushered into the room. The Assemblyman was pale and looked as though he hadn't slept, but his chin was up and his eyes were steady. Nothing had broken in the press yet and he still had his finger in the dike. He sent a hostile glare at the Scotsman, said civilly to Carey, "Yes, Commissioner? Pat said you wanted to talk to me. Here I am."

He sat down in the indicated chair, crossed well-tailored legs and lit a cigarette. He stuck to his story that he hadn't killed Sara Hazard and that he knew nothing pertinent concerning her death. When she put the heat on him the night she slipped away from the St. Vrain party, he had agreed to pay her a thousand dollars. But he couldn't raise it until he got hold of Tommy Gordon, one of his clients, who ran the Abelard and who was the only one he could think of who could produce that much money in a hurry. He didn't want to brace Pat. He went to the Abelard and Tommy did produce.

Dropping in at the St. Vrain party on the way, he arranged to meet Sara Hazard at the Abelard after three. The Abelard was on Fifty-eighth Street near the river. He waited for her a long while. When she didn't show up he left the café, started to walk home and ran into the crowd on the river bank above the submerged car.

The Commissioner said, "I see." The Scotsman didn't say anything. Abelard's was jammed between 1 a.m. and the closing hour on a Sunday morning. A herd of elephants could trumpet through it unnoticed.

"Were you alone, Mr. Somers, or was there someone with you?" McKee asked.

"I was alone," Clifford Somers said.

McKee smiled cynically. The smile touched off the Assemblyman's repressed rage. He got to his feet and said in a shaking voice, "I've told you the truth. You can make the worst of it if you like. Why don't you devote your attention to someone else for a change, Inspector? Steven Hazard knew that his wife was a low-down blackmailing bitch. Pat told him to his face that night, the night of the St. Vrain party. Where was Hazard between one o'clock and six the next morning?"

He shook a finger at McKee. "And what about that gun that Sara Hazard carried around with her? I know she had a gun."

"The gun," McKee said musingly, "yes. I wonder where that gun is now."

It was Clifford Somers's turn to smile. He looked intently at the Scotsman. He said, very slowly, "Why don't you ask Steven Hazard?"

Chapter Ten
THE WAREHOUSE

TYPEWRITERS were clacking and men were moving to and fro adding to the rapidly accumulating material on case No. 22-683 that had been changed from "closed" to "open" when McKee reached the office.

Seated behind his desk in the long narrow inner room to which he had come from his interview with Police Commissioner Carey, McKee ran rapidly through reports. He paused at one headed Detective Charles Mathers. Mathers was among the men combing the neighborhood of the Hazard apartment for any stray facts about the night of the murder.

They already knew that Margot St. Vrain's fiancé, Euen Firth, had driven Sara Hazard home from the party in his cream-colored roadster. Joe Williams, porter and handyman at the Franklin Place apartment building, added to their knowledge. After Sara Hazard left him that night Euen Firth remained in front of the apartment for some time. According to the porter he seemed to be dozing. When Mrs. Hazard's maid, Eva Prentice, passed along the pavement on her way home, Mr. Firth had called out to her, mistaking her for her mistress. She just stared at him and continued on her way. Right afterward he drove off.

The porter placed the time as around three, say four or five minutes before Mrs. Hazard left the Franklin Place apartment on her last trip anywhere. Euen Firth, Margot

St. Vrain's prospective husband, had been remarkably at-
tentive and kind to leave his fiancé's party and to see Sara
Hazard home. The Scotsman decided to go into that last
evening at the St. Vrains more thoroughly.

He pulled the phone toward him. A manservant at Euen
Firth's apartment on Fifty-ninth Street South said that Mr.
Firth was out of town and wasn't expected back until Tues-
day. Same result when he called Margot St. Vrain. They
were probably week-ending somewhere. He despatched
men to the penthouse to talk to the servants.

Steven Hazard had gone to the Tarrytown factory and
wouldn't be back in the city until evening. McKee wanted
to talk to him about the missing gun and the maid.

The Royal Employment Agency, through which Sara
Hazard had hired Eva, gave her home address as Hempstead, Long Island, care of Mrs. John Hansen, 234 West-
erly Avenue. The telephone number was Hempstead
6794-3. A call there got no answer. McKee sent men to
Hempstead, sent more men touring the pawn shops in case
the maid had tried to cash in on the stolen jewelry. Too
early yet to broadcast an alarm.

That was about all on Eva for the moment, until they
knew more. According to the descriptions of her that he
had picked up, she was a shrewd hard-headed girl with
eyes wide open. Servants were excellent sources of information. Sometimes they knew almost as much about their
employers' private lives as their employers knew themselves. If the maid was innocent of any hand in Sara Hazard's murder, if her crime was confined to theft and if she
could be induced to come forward, she ought to be a gold
mine.

He turned his attention to the missing gun, scribbled

"caliber? make? classification?" on a sheet of yellow paper in front of him. It was difficult to start searching for a weapon whose only description consisted of the word "gun." Neverthless, he determined to have a try at it.

If, as he was more and more inclined to think, the weapon had been used as a bludgeon with which to knock Sara Hazard out before she plunged into the river, it might be lying in the mud at the bottom. It might have been discarded, thrown into a sewer opening, the nearest ashcan, or it might still be in possession of the killer.

McKee sighed. Cover the first two possibilities. Tedious work but it had to be done. The gun was assuming constantly increasing importance as the single material clue.

The telephone rang. Miss Dodd was at the other end of the wire. Mary Dodd said, "I'd like to see you, Inspector. There's something I want to tell you. Where can I talk to you and when?"

McKee's answer was prompt. "Right now. At your house, if that's convenient."

Miss Dodd said that would be splendid and McKee hung up and reached for his hat.

The October afternoon was chilly. Mary Dodd was standing in front of a log fire under the wide mantel when he entered the long living room of the house on Seventy-third Street. She looked tired, but a measure of serenity had returned to her. She gave him her hand, a slender white hand, the nails pleasantly unlacquered. Her deep blue eyes were steady. The room, the house, were full of mementoes of the late Dr. Dodd. Her existence with her father must have been quiet, studious. Kit Blaketon had changed all that.

Mary Dodd went directly to the point. Seated in a chair

opposite McKee, she said, "I feel there's something I ought to tell you, Inspector. I don't know whether or not it's relevant, or whether it has anything to do with Sara's death. But about ten days before, I found that it was gone."

The playing of the record the night before had changed her whole attitude. She was no longer quite so guarded. Her tone was freer, less constrained.

McKee said pleasantly, "What was gone, Miss Dodd?"

"The pistol," she answered. "It was in the drawer that morning because I saw it. It wasn't there that evening. Come, I'll show you."

She led McKee into the library beyond the living room. It still held intact Dr. Dodd's magnificent collection of books on applied psychology. Mary Dodd paused at the massive table in the middle of the shadowy room. She showed him the drawer in which the gun had been kept, a gun bought originally because of burglaries in the neighborhood.

McKee asked her its make and caliber. It was an automatic Colt .32.

Mary Dodd said, "Sara came to tea that afternoon. Before she left, she came in here to write a note. She was alone in here. Cliff and Kit and myself remained in the living room."

"What did you think when you missed the weapon?" McKee asked.

Mary Dodd shrugged. "It didn't worry me much at the time. I really didn't give it much thought at all. It might have been mislaid, or someone might have moved it. But since yesterday when you were here...Well..."

She pushed an antique silver bracelet with tiny primitive figures hanging from it, higher on her rounded white arm.

The little figures danced, sending out a tinkle. Her forehead was puckered in a frown.

"I began to wonder. The maid, Eva Prentice, Inspector, was a thief and was sly; the sort of person who would listen outside doors. Knowing what we know about Sara"—a flush colored Mary Dodd's cheeks and the nostrils of her long, delicate nose flared a little—"couldn't it be possible that Sara took that gun and the maid knew she had it? If that's true, could it be possible that Sara discovered that Eva Prentice was stealing from her, that she threatened the maid with the police, and then that Eva Prentice killed her?"

Her oblique reference to the purple patch in Clifford Somers's past filled her with shame, distress. It would. Her life had been more or less sequestered and she was a proud woman. No doubt now that she hated Sara Hazard as much as she liked Steven. She had known that Sara threatened Kit Blaketon's happiness. One stone would have brought down three fine-feathered friends; Sara's elimination would have released Steven Hazard, Kit Blaketon and Cliff Somers.

He considered her suggestion thoughtfully. It had its points. One of them was the rather obvious attempt to remove suspicion from the people Mary Dodd was interested in and throw it toward the missing maid.

They were back in the living room. The Inspector was out of his range of vision when the door opened and Steven Hazard came in. Hazard greeted Mary Dodd with affection, not looking at her directly, ignoring her warning gesture. "Lord, it's good to be here." He tossed his hat and gloves into a chair. "Well, I gave that damn detective who's on my heels a run for his money. I had to go up to the factory this afternoon. Didn't know if I could make it for dinner or not. But I got through earlier than I thought. I want to talk to you, Mary. Gosh, it's good to . . ." He turned his head, saw the Scotsman, and pulled up short. The light went out of his face.

McKee bowed. "You're just the man I want to see, Mr. Hazard. I've been trying to get hold of you since half past two."

Hazard threw himself into a corner of the couch, stretched his long legs in front of him, thrust his hands into his pockets and surveyed the Inspector. His long strong face was grim. Colliding with McKee was quite evidently not a pleasure to him.

The Inspector put his question about the missing gun, gave its source. Hazard's answer was forceful almost explosive.

"I don't care what Cliff Somers said. He's got a hell of a nerve. I don't know anything about Sara and any gun. I never saw her with one, never knew she had one in her possession. You're talking Chinese as far as I'm concerned and I'm not good at languages."

The Scotsman looked at Hazard thoughtfully. No dice. He hadn't expected much from Hazard himself. The maid, the missing gun, the ungrieving husband. He would have to try it from another angle. McKee left the house.

Late the next afternoon Captain Pierson and the Inspector stepped out of the freight elevator on the fifth floor of the Plymouth Warehouse, where the Hazard household goods, such as they were, had been stored. Twenty-four hours had produced no basic changes. The search for the missing Colt .32 was so far a blank. So was the search for the missing maid.

The two officials had declined the services of the attendant and were alone. The upper reaches of the warehouse
were completely devoid of life. A long narrow alley ran
away from the freight elevator between stalls of various
sizes. They were piled with the furniture of dismantled
homes. Chairs and tables and statuary and pianos and sofas
and huge crates reared themselves in vague, distorted
shapes in semi-darkness. The quiet was somnolent, drowsy.
The air, at the correct temperature, seemed stale.

The Hazard cubicle was number thirty-six. McKee and
Pierson started along a side aisle. Their feet made a noise
and when Pierson spoke, his voice echoed loudly. He said,
"It's a hell of a walk. Twenty-three, twenty-four, must be
round the next corner."

They started around the corner. Footsteps, not their own
beat a sudden rapid tattoo. They decreased in volume. They
were made by a man running away in a hurry. Off to the
left beyond the dark rampart of the last stall a door closed.

McKee paused beside the Hazard cubicle, threw a quick
look. The Hazard furniture there was disarranged. The
drawer of a table was open, there were papers on the floor.
He said over his shoulder as he sprinted for the door that
had closed, "Stay here, Pierson, I'll be back."

He ran lightly and swiftly down the five flights of stairs.
There was no one on them. The door at the bottom led
directly into the office. McKee opened it cautiously and
looked out. His brows rose. Two men were standing in
the middle of the floor staring at each other. They were
Steven Hazard and John St. Vrain, the radio announcer.

There was wariness in their mutual scrutiny. St. Vrain
said, lighting a cigarette, "Hello, Hazard, where did you

spring from?"

Steven Hazard waved vaguely. "I sprang through the door."

McKee noted that he didn't say *which* door as he continued, "Yourself, St. Vrain?"

The radio announcer said easily, "I've been looking over some junk of mine here."

There was antagonism and covert watchfulness under the casual interchange. St. Vrain offered Hazard a cigarette. Hazard refused, took out one of his own brand. St. Vrain held a match to it.

Hazard said, "Thanks."

St. Vrain said, "Well. So long. Say hello to Cristie for me," and turned toward the door.

Hazard threw down his smoke, rubbed it out with the side of his shoe, and watched him go.

Half a minute later, standing in the embrasure of the doorway outside, McKee saw a curious and interesting sight. St. Vrain was a good distance down the block, walking rapidly. Steven Hazard was well in the rear, but was following St. Vrain. As the latter disappeared around the corner, Steven Hazard broke into a sharp trot. The two men were not alone. Slipping along in the rear, Todhunter covered them both.

Back in the office later, McKee examined the afternoon's catch. The man whose search of the Hazard cubicle had been interrupted by their own arrival could have been either the radio announcer or Steven Hazard. The clerk said that both men had entered the warehouse before they themselves had got there and that both were upstairs, where they had a right to be since they both had storage cubicles. The clerk didn't know which man had come down first.

His only concern was with the opening of the front door which was announced by the ringing of a bell.

There was one item which might be significant, and might be chance. John St. Vrain had rented space in the Plymouth Warehouse on the day following McKee's own official appearance on the scene.

Was the interrupted search of the Hazard booth an attempt to get possession of the missing gun for purposes of removing it permanently from circulation? Of the two men, Steven Hazard's conduct was the more ambiguous. Why had he been trailing Johnny St. Vrain? There was the girl angle, of course. The radio announcer had taken Cristie Lansing out quite a bit before the intrusion of Hazard into the picture.

McKee returned restlessly to the major problem. Missing gun, missing maid, Steven Hazard. Three points of a triangle. Resolve the riddle they covered and the rest would come.

Located in a two-family house in Hempstead, Eva Prentice's sister professed complete ignorance of Eva's whereabouts. She said she hadn't heard from or seen Eva since the previous July. The Scotsman sat erect in his chair. The time for cover, the advantage that cover gave their own work was over. Watch everybody, with special attention to Hazard, and find Eva Prentice at all costs.

He reached for the phone, called Headquarters and ordered a general alarm broadcast for the maid.

Chapter Eleven
JOURNEY AT NIGHT

CHRISTIE LANSING stood at one of the long windows in the living room of Margot St. Vrain's penthouse looking out over the roofs of the city. The light had begun to fade. Night was coming.

She held the key in one hand, the sheet of cheap note paper in the other. The envelope containing them had been slipped under the door with several other letters five minutes earlier. Bewilderment, and little stabs of fear, the fear that never quite left her these days, were going through her in waves. She lifted the letter with fingers that were stiff, unwieldy, and read it again. It said:

Miss Cristie Lansing, go to 503A East 21st Street tonight at 8:45 sharp. Open the door of the basement apartment 1A with the key please find enclosed. You will find out something you ought to know about Sara Hazard's death. Don't let yourself be seen. When you get into the apartment, go behind the screen that is in front of the wash basin. And watch. Well wisher.

Conflicting emotions clashed sharply inside of her, curiosity, dread, indecision, terrified surmise. She threw the letter from her. If only she could go to Steven. But she couldn't. Steven had his own burden to bear; she had hers.

That he was bearing a burden which was becoming heavier and heavier had shown itself quite clearly in his actions, his manner, in the expression of his face when he thought he was unobserved, in his sudden silences, the peculiar look that flashed occasionally into the clarity of his eyes.

She couldn't get close to him. The oneness between them was gone. It had begun to disappear with the advent of that tall, cold, clever Inspector with his endless questions about Sara and Sara's death.

Cristie closed her eyes, shutting out Sara just as, at the back of her mind, she closed a door sharply on the blackness that lay behind it. The police weren't going to be able to discover anything real. There wasn't anything to discover. She had told herself that at the beginning. She repeated it firmly now, drawing on her courage, her strength.

She looked at the key. It was small and flat, with the usual notches. If she used it, what would it reveal? Would it deepen the terror that she had so far been able to keep under control, or would it place certainty on top of what were only frightened questions as yet? Who or what would she find within the room it would unlock? It might be a trap, a device to get her into a spot where she would *have* to talk. She wouldn't go. It would be too dangerous.

She turned from the window, walked the length of the rug, paused beside the piano and stared at herself in the long mirror beyond it. She drew back, crushed herself into the curve of the polished rosewood. How dreadful she looked. Those shadows under her eyes, the way her eyes were sunk in her head, her color—even her lips were pale.

She went into her bedroom, put on lipstick with bold forceful strokes, used unaccustomed rouge, dusted her skin with powder, ran a comb through her hair. Whatever happened, she mustn't show anything. She returned to the living room, picked up the letter, and the envelope, tore them both into shreds, watched them blaze in the fireplace, disappear. She took the key from the table where she had flung it, started for the bathroom, paused as Margot's maid, Emma, came in and asked what she'd like for dinner. She slipped the key into her pocket.

Dinner was early. She ate alone. Margot was in Chicago on business. All during the meal, over coffee in the living room later, she kept up that fierce inner argument. Prudence said, *Stay where you are; don't move; don't do anything; wait.* But another part of her said, *It is better to know, you can fight the known, it's the unknown that holds the real menace.* She went backward and forward, up and down, trying to balance in nightmare.

If she did make up her mind to go . . . She threw a cloak over her shoulders and went out on the terrace. Propping her elbows on the railing she leaned over, and searched the street below with her eyes. Yes, he was there, the man Margot had pointed out to her on Monday evening, when she returned unexpectedly to the apartment on her way to Chicago. Margot had told her not to say anything about her flying visit. A vague shadow of wonder flitted across her mind at Margot's desire for secrecy. She had said she didn't want anyone to know she was in New York or she would be inundated with calls, and she had to get on to Chicago. Margot had told her something else, a way to get out of the building without being seen.

A moon was coming up in the East. It topped the serrated horizon, hung there a moment, a shining silver dish, suspended above a pinnacle. Cristie looked at it. Freedom and the possibility of escape if she went, if the cards fell right. Nothing ventured, nothing gained. She crushed out her cigarette, re-entered the penthouse and got her hat and coat.

She didn't get off at the main floor. She ran the self-service elevator down to the basement where she emerged into a corridor flanked with doors. Margot had said the door labeled "Furnace Room." Cristie passed "Laundry," "Parcels," went round a turn. There it was. She opened the door to the furnace room, negotiated oil tanks and asbestos-jacketed monsters and entered another large cement tunnel with various doors opening out of it. She must be under the apartment to the left. The basement there led her in turn to the one beyond and to the one beyond that. All four apartment houses were the property of one corporation and while they were under different names they were operated as a unit. When she finally emerged into the air she was on the avenue instead of on the side street where the watching detective still loitered opposite the main and apparently the only entrance to the penthouse.

Cristie hailed a cab. She kept the fur collar of her coat up and the rim of her hat, a wide dark brown hat, well down over her forehead. She rode as far as Second Avenue and Twenty-third Street, dismissed the cab and started to walk south.

At Twenty-first she turned east again. So far the neighborhood hadn't been bad. It began to degenerate rapidly. Boarded and abandoned tenements, poor, meanly lighted shops loomed up. The address she sought was between Avenues A and B.

She paused in the gloom outside the five-story red brick tenement with its dingy windows, broken steps and sagged railings. The note said the basement. Entrance to the basement was to the right of the front door. There had once been a gate. The gate was gone. She descended three steps to a door in shadow under the porch, opened the door and stepped into a long narrow dimly-lighted hallway. An odor of ancient goulash, of dirt, decayed vegetable matter, and strong soap pervaded the heavy air. There was no one in sight.

Cristie walked steadily to the door of Apartment 1A. Her nerves were steel tight. She fitted the key that had been sent to her into the lock without a tremor, and pushed open the door.

The apartment was in blackness. She halted, listened for a sound. There was none. She slipped inside, closed the door softly behind her and groped until she found the light switch. As the room sprang into brightness she saw that her informant had been accurate. The screen was there in the far corner. The room contained, besides, a wide double bed, a bureau, two comfortable shabby armchairs, a card table, a portable tin ice-box and a meager assortment of crockery and glasses in the bottom of the washstand.

Cristie switched off the light. Crossing the floor she stepped behind the screen, propped herself against the wall and waited.

One of the faucets in the basin leaked. The drip, drip, drip, against the dull pianissimo of the city that seemed a thousand miles away marked off endless spaces in a limbo without boundaries. Outside in the street a horse clumped by dragging a creaking huckster's cart. A child cried distantly. The water dripped a little faster, slowed again. It went drip, drip, drip, and then *drip* on a long note.

The exhaustion of stretched nerves made her faintly drowsy. Her head ached. She snapped erect at the sound of metal against metal. Someone outside in the hall was fitting a key into the lock of apartment 1A. The door opened, closed. The light flashed on.

Cristie cowered back against the rough plaster of the wall. Just for an instant fortitude deserted her. She felt weak, ill. A man was standing with his back to the closed door. His eyes were fastened on the washstand that contained the crockery. They were narrow and bright and terrible in the intensity of their motionless gaze. The long strong face between upturned coat collar and gray fedora wore a look that Cristie had never seen on it before, a look that was savage, ruthless. The man was Steven.

Cristie forced down an involuntary cry. She leaned forward until she was opposite a slit between two leaves of the screen. Through this slit she watched Steven Hazard, the man who had suddenly become a stranger to her.

The shades of the room were drawn. Steven moved across the floor to the green washstand. He got down on one knee. He reached in and with the surety of one certain of his goal, pushed aside a pile of plates, moved a sugar bowl and lifted the cover of a vegetable dish. He took something out of the dish and replaced the lid. He stood up, his back was toward Cristie. She couldn't see the object he held in his hands. He turned, and she did.

Light from the unshaded bulb in the ceiling fell on the squat black automatic gripped in Steven's fingers. Cristie's heart pumped blood furiously, deafeningly. The gun the Inspector had questioned Steven about, all knowledge of which he had denied, the gun that had been in Sara's possession on the night she died and that the police were searching for—Steven had it. Steven had known all the time where it was.

She couldn't take her eyes away. She wanted to, but she

couldn't. Steven's movements were slow, deliberate. He
stared at the weapon. He took a clean handkerchief out
of the breast pocket of his tweed jacket. He enclosed the
gun in its folds. His sinewy brown hands worked busily.
And then, all at once, he stopped doing anything. His head
was up. He was looking toward the door. So fast that Cristie
could barely follow, he was across to the bed, had folded
the covers back, had lifted the far corner of the mattress
and had slipped the weapon out of sight. Returning the
covers to their former position, he slid to the switch and
jabbed off the light. As blackness came down again, Cristie
heard the door close.

Her breast was an anvil and someone was pounding on
it with a hammer. She couldn't think, couldn't even feel.
She knew only one thing. She had to get out of there and
she had to get out instantly. Every step through the blackness was a searing ordeal. She reached the door at last,
turned the knob with icy fingers. She was in the hall with
the door closed when she heard someone coming down
the steps from the street into the basement.

Cristie glanced around. There was no way of escape.
Then she saw the staircase leading to the floor above. She
ran toward it, up its worn treads, along the hallway above
and without being stopped, out onto the high stoop and
down into the dim night street.

Cristie didn't go to sleep until almost morning, and only
then because she took a sedative. When she woke at nine
she thought at first that the whole horrible experience
hadn't actually happened, that it was nothing but a bad
dream. Then realization rushed through her, detailed,
cruel, biting. The secret door at the back of her mind was

wide open now. The fear that lurked there ranged the outer regions of her consciousness, misshapen, monstrous, terrible.

Every minute of every hour of the long day was an intolerable effort; getting up, eating breakfast, answering her maid's smiling good morning, going to her drawing board, trying to do the sketches for Lyons. At two she went out for a walk in an effort to obtain surcease if only for a few minutes from her own bitter problem.

The sight of normal people, guiltless people, going unconcernedly about their own affairs, deepened the taste of gall on her tongue and drove her indoors again. At half past four she.rang Steven. They were to have had dinner together. She couldn't face it. His voice gave her a little shock because it sounded the same; there was no change in it. She had somehow or other expected there to be a change. Steven was a very good actor. Swallowing around a constriction in her throat, she said, "Hello, Steven? I'm afraid I can't make it for dinner tonight. No. I feel rotten. I guess I've got a cold coming on."

Steven expressed his concern, and before she could stop him said he'd be right up. The connection was broken. Cristie steeled herself. She took a shower, changed, and put on fresh make-up. Outlining the curve of her mouth in the dressing-table mirror she marveled at herself with a sort of dull wonder. There was no outward mark. She looked much as usual. It seemed incredible after what had come and gone.

When Steven arrived she was at her drawing board again. She smiled at him brightly, accepted his kiss, cut it short by upsetting a jar of chinese white. Deception was easier than it looked. After the first few minutes she heard herself answering Steven in normal tones. The maid brought in cocktails. The drinks helped.

She was sipping the second one when the door bell rang and the maid ushered Inspector McKee and another man into the room. The latter was Kent, the Homicide Squad stenographer. Cristie put her glass down slowly and carefully. There was a change in the Inspector's manner. Carelessness had dropped from his tall, lean, casually tweeded figure. His dark saturnine face was modeled in grave planes and there was no smile in his eyes.

Steven was on his feet.

"Mr. Hazard," McKee said, "I believe you made a little expedition last night." His voice was cold, even, as he went on with his indictment. "You left your club at about eight-thirty. You took a cab to Grand Central. You got out of the cab and went down in the East Side subway to Fourteenth Street. You took another cab to First Avenue and Twentieth Street. You dismissed the cab there, crossed to Avenue A and entered the basement of 503A East Twenty-first Street. You went into room 1A at the back of the hall. You were in the room for about two minutes. You didn't succeed in shaking off the men following you. One detective took you back to your club. The other, Detective Schwartz, searched the room after you left. Any explanation to offer, Mr. Hazard, of your desire to keep your expedition and its objective a secret?"

The words were concise, came like leaden balls out of a mold. Cristie crushed herself into a corner of the big couch, hands, feet and knees together. She held her breath waiting for Steven to answer.

"None," he said.

The Scotsman leaned toward him, the last trace of conciliation gone. He said slowly, "Mr. Hazard, that room was rented and occupied by Eva Prentice, your former maid. You went there to collect something, something she had in her keeping. You went there to get this..."

The Inspector's hand went into his pocket, came out holding the squat automatic that Sara had slipped into the pocket of her ermine cape on the night of Margot's party, that had been gone when Steven left Margot's room; the gun that Steven had hidden under the mattress in the tenement on Twenty-first Street.

The Inspector continued implacably. "There are no fingerprints on this gun, Mr. Hazard. You wiped them off before you hid it under the mattress of Eva Prentice's bed, didn't you?" McKee waited.

The stenographer's pencil was poised. The only word Kent had down from Hazard was the word "none." Spreading pallor crept along Steven's white jaw.

"I don't know anything about that gun," he said in measured tones. "I didn't wipe any fingerprints off it. I never saw it before in my life."

Cristie sat very still. Her breathing had stopped. She wanted to stop her ears. She had to keep on listening. McKee tapped the gun lying on his outstretched palm. He said, "Mr. Hazard, you may stand on your privileges if you wish. You can refuse to answer any further questions without the advice of counsel. I am convinced that on the night she died your wife received a blow at the base of the brain that fractured her skull. This gun has been taken apart and gone over. The surfaces are clean, it's true, but the surfaces aren't all. Blood and fragments of blonde hair were found in the crevices, blood that corresponds with the same group as your wife's was recorded in the autopsy report. This is the gun that actually killed your wife."

The noise in Cristie's ears had mounted to a roar. If Steven answered, she didn't hear his answer. She simply recorded with some part of her brain that continued to function independently that the stenographer closed his book—and then that, somehow or other, all three men were gone and the room was empty of them and she was alone.

Chapter Twelve
THE VOICE

CRISTIE WENT to bed early. She was spent, exhausted, needed no drug. She fell asleep almost at once, woke some time later on and glanced at the luminous dial of the clock on the table beside the bed. It was only a little after half past eleven. She had slept for less than two hours. It seemed like a span of years spent journeying in distant lands across unnumbered continents.

She turned her head listlessly on the pillow, looked through the open window and rose on one elbow. The maid had gone to bed before Cristie, but there was someone in the living room. Reflected light from its illuminated interior made tall spears of the iron fence around the visible portion of the terrace. Who was in there? It must be Margot. Margot must have come home.

Cristie lay still for a moment, watching the glow on the long grill. Margot was hard-headed, capable, efficient. Impossible to tell her everything, but there were some things on which you could ask her advice. Cristie hesitated, then threw the covers back. She put on the dark blue flannel robe thrown over a chair, slipped into mules and opened her door. The hall was dark. The glass doors to the living room, forty feet away, were ajar.

"Margot," she called, and started forward.

Before she had taken half a dozen steps, the living room lights went out. Standing motionless in the sudden blanketing darkness, Cristie listened. She couldn't hear anything except—it was absurd—a faint sound like the galloping of little horses. Then after a moment the front door opened and closed.

Cristie was trembling. Terror was back in her again. She stilled it with a hand at her heart, found the hall switch, pushed it up, walked resolutely into the living room and turned on the lights there.

The room was empty. There was no evidence of an intruder. Everything was in order. Cristie frowned at Margot's immense chromium and leather desk. She was still shaking.

It couldn't have been Margot because Margot would have recognized her voice. The only other people who might have keys were Johnny and Euen Firth. But surely they too would have... She folded the dressing gown tightly around her, compressed her lips. Someone had undoubtedly effected an entrance to the penthouse, someone who had withdrawn with stealth and with despatch at her call. Whoever it was had come there with an objective: Her eyes went swiftly around the room again. Did the intruder get what he was after?

She made herself stop trembling. She mustn't lose control. She was going to need every ounce of it for the long ordeal that lay ahead. No use trying to think things out tonight, or to plan. That was for tomorrow when her brain was rested and her nerves were in better shape.

She went out into the foyer, tried the door, found that it was locked and picked up a small Windsor chair. She hung the chair over the knob so that any further attempt at entry would produce a loud crash, and returned to her room, and to bed.

Rest—she had to have rest, and sleep and the healing of forgetfulness, if only for a few hours, to refill the springs of her courage. But sleep was done with her for the remainder of the night, except in broken snatches that were filled with tumbling nightmares. It wasn't until daylight came that she dropped into oblivion.

It was at half past two that afternoon that she put in a call for Steven at the office of National Motors. Would Steven be there? She had to see him. Her fear hadn't gone with the night. If anything, it had deepened. But she was no longer undecided, wavering. Strength had returned to her. She had pushed the doubts, the fears, the ugliness, the black uncertainties into the back of her mind, had closed a door firmly on them. The past was past. Nothing could be done about that. The present and the future remained. If they played it right they might still win through. Not to happiness—she didn't attempt to deceive herself for a moment—happiness was not for them, but they might avert the worst.

Her pulses leaped when Steven answered. One barrier surmounted. Steven said he would be at the penthouse at about a quarter of six. The rest of the afternoon dragged interminably and then he was there, in the room with her, taking her in his arms and kissing her with hungry passion. She released herself with a small shaky laugh. She turned to the fire and picked up the tongs.

"What did they do to you, Steven?" she asked. "I mean, last night? About the gun—and that maid?"

She was aware of Steven's eyes on the curve of her cheek, her bent head, traveling over the satin folds of the blue house gown sweeping to the floor. There was a pause before he said in a different voice, a brusque harsh voice, "You're not to worry about that, Cristie. The police have nothing on me, nothing whatever. McKee knows it. He's too shrewd a man not to know. They have absolutely no evidence to tie the possession of that gun to me. In order to do any good, make a charge stick, they'd have to put it in my hands, watch me wipe fingerprints from it."

Cristie didn't turn. She kept on staring into the flames. *"They would have to place it in my hands, see me wipe fingerprints from it."* A sickness swept through her, dimming her vision, taking the sight from her eyes. Her hands and feet were cold, clammy. For just an instant she had an almost overwhelming temptation to turn to Steven and tell him the truth, not only the truth about the gun, but the truth of what had taken place on that black August night when Sara died, or rather in the early hours of that morning.

She fought her weakness down. Not that way. Some time perhaps, but not yet. It would ruin everything. She put a fresh birch log on the fire, returned the tongs to the stand and swung around. Steven was regarding her intently from under his thick black brows. The angle of his jaw was sharp. His eyes gleamed palely. The muscles of his broad-shouldered, narrow-hipped, long-legged body were tight.

She thought—Steven, lying. He doesn't trust me; I don't trust him. And then it came to her. Not joy, not rapture, but a realization of the facts that lay under these things. She loved Steven, she would always love him, no matter what had happened, no matter what was happening now, no matter what was going to happen.

Going to happen. The words acted as a spur. She raised her head. "Steven," she said, "there's something I want you to do for me."

"Yes, Cristie?" Steven had been far away. His face softened. He smiled at her.

Cristie returned the smile. Her own was a little uncertain, a little tremulous. "Steven," she said, "will you marry me? Now? Right away?"

She didn't wait for him to come to her. As she spoke she went to him, put her arms around his neck and pressed her cheek tightly against his.

Steven didn't answer her at once, didn't respond to the pressure of her clinging. She could feel the struggle going on inside of him. She slid her cheek around, found his lips.

"Yes, Steven. Yes," she whispered, drawing back. "Don't you see? It's the only way. The only way to ..."

Steven was still holding her. He put her from him. "The only way to what?"

Cristie let her lashes fall, buried her face in his breast. She couldn't tell him, couldn't put into words the things she knew, the things that made it imperative that they should become man and wife and so gain the haven of immunity the legal tie offered. No wife could be forced to take the witness stand against her husband and no husband could be forced to testify against his wife.

She lifted her face, said, looking up into his, putting urgency into her tone, "I'm frightened, Steven. I want protection. I want someone to lean on. If we're married, if you're my husband, I won't be so—so alone."

It was only this plea, repeated again and again, that finally induced Steven to consider her proposal. She took advantage of his tentative weakening, made him comfortable on a chair beside the hearth, mixed a drink, settled herself on a puff beside him and began overriding the objections he raised, one after another.

"We're being watched," he said. "If we take such a step at this juncture—why, look, Cristie ..."

She swept that aside. There were ways, there must be ways. She started putting forth suggestions. Her excitement kindled an answering spark in Steven. He sat up. He lit a cigarette and reached for a second drink. His color was better and his eyes brighter.

"By God, it might be done at that."

Cristie drew the puff closer to his knees, laid her clasped hands on them. They began to talk in low eager voices. They went on talking for a long while.

It was nine o'clock before Steven left the penthouse. The envelope containing the ticket arrived by messenger at half past eleven the next morning. Cristie ate a leisurely luncheon. There was plenty of time.

At two she changed into a dark plaid suit with a plaid topcoat, selected a hat. She chose a bright red one with a black wing on it that stood up jauntily on her soft dark hair. She checked over the contents of her purse, made sure that her toothbrush was in it, and powder and her lipstick and what money she had. Dressed and ready to leave the penthouse, she pulled open a drawer of the highboy, got out a tan beret that matched the lining of the plaid topcoat, stowed it, neatly folded, in a capacious pocket and picked up her gloves.

She went down quite openly in the self-service elevator, got out at the main floor. The elevator was just inside the door. As she went through them and down the steps she watched a stoutish man in a gray hat and brown overcoat detach himself from interested contemplation of a flight of pigeons and saunter after her along the street.

She hailed a cab at the corner, saw with satisfaction that

the gray-hatted, brown-coated detective was doing like-
wise. At Eighty-sixth Street, she took the East Side subway uptown.

The stations fled by. Immersed in her magazine she was
aware of her shadow resting bulkily reading a newspaper
beyond a stout woman with a baby a few feet away. At
161st Street, she got out, went down the steps. The Yankee
Stadium reared itself above her. A sudden roar burst from
the hidden crowd within the huge enclosure. She walked
to the right field entrance. A sign said "Texas A. & M. vs.
Fordham" in big bold letters. She gave her ticket to the
man at the gate, walked up a ramp and consulted the stub.

A scarlet-coated attendant escorted her to her seat. Cristie
settled back after a sideways glance established her detective
settling himself in a seat ten rows behind.

It was working out exactly as they had planned it. The
second half had begun. The stands were packed. Alternate
sunlight and shadow drifted across the white-lined playing
field and the 69,000 spectators. Both Texas and Fordham
were big draws. The crowds had turned out for them.
Bright colors, excitement, its focal point those twenty-two
jerseyed figures, running, tangling, swooping, darting, out
on the field. The throng followed them breathlessly, surging to its feet as a halfback cut off tackle and got in the open
on Fordham's thirty-five for a gain of seventeen yards
and another first down.

It was a tightly fought game. To her astonishment,
Cristie found herself caught up in its thrills. The acting she
was going to have to do oughtn't to be difficult. The third
quarter ended with the teams still locked in a tie. The
fourth quarter began.

Fordham put on a late drive. Plunging deeper and deeper

into Texas territory, they reached the Texas twenty-yard line. They were on the twelve, then the eight. Texas recovered a fumble. A groan went up from the Fordham side of the huge stadium. There was a yell as Fordham intercepted a forward pass on its own forty-seven.

A collective gasp of suspense broke from the 69,000 people. Cristie glanced at the big clock above the scoreboard. Two minutes to go. Would Fordham make it? Would she make it? A chill went through her that had nothing to do with the frosty wind or the sudden grayness of a passing cloud.

First down. A loss. Second, only four yards this time. Time out for a substitution. One minute to go. And then it came. The Fordham man faded back, waited and threw a prodigious pass. Dead on the run the rangy end plucked it out of the air, shot forward alone and went over the Texas goal line for a touchdown.

The kick was bad but nobody cared. Only thirty-five seconds to play. Everyone was standing now. Cristie stood too. Her vigilant trailer had moved up closer. There was just time for a kick-off. The gun sounded and the crowd · went mad.

Cristie was caught up in the laughing, cheering, riotous mob. If she had wanted to she couldn't have freed herself. She didn't want to. Already the detective in the gray hat was separated from her by hundreds of shoving men and women. She let herself be pushed this way and that indifferently. She was bent on other things. No one noticed the slim girl in the plaid outfit and the scarlet hat turn into an entirely different figure. The red hat pulled from her head, the beret slipped into its place, the plaid coat was reversible. She had to struggle to get it inside out and button its tan exterior neatly down the front.

The goal posts trembled and went down. A cheer rose and the crowd milled toward the various exits arguing and expostulating, replaying the game. Cristie searched the faces nearest her. The detective's wasn't among them. Careful to remain embedded in that flowing tide of humanity she was carried out of the stadium along the street and up the hill to the Independent subway station.

The station was packed but she was able to crush her way into an early downtown express. The crowd had thinned a great deal by the time she reached the West Fourth Street station but she wasn't afraid now.

As she walked across Christopher Street, exultation made her a little light-headed so that she forgot for a moment the grimmer aspects of the adventure that still lay ahead. It couldn't fail now. What she had done, Steven would be repeating in a different shape. They had gone over every move carefully. He would do what he did every Saturday, lunch, then back to his club to loaf for a couple of hours. Then the game with a seat in another section. During the goal post rush he would have shaken off his man.

She turned the corner. It was there, the little black sedan that Steven had ordered and that had been parked at his direction in front of the old brown church on Hudson Street, opposite the opening of Grove. It was the car that was to carry them south to the little town that Steven had selected.

Light from the sun sinking in the West flared out on either side of the square church tower silhouetting its bulk sharply. The sedan was empty. Steven had not yet arrived. Cristie walked to and fro in front of the big, red brick school, silent and deserted on Saturday afternoon.

After a little while she glanced at her watch. It was only twenty-five minutes past five. The game had ended at twenty of five. She had gotten down fast. Steven might be having trouble. She mustn't permit herself to become impatient.

She went on walking. An occasional taxi flitted by, buses; an occasional man or woman entered or left the houses along the street. The shadows lengthened. The wind grew colder. Cristie forced herself to go south as far as the drugstore on the corner. She could still see the sedan, empty, waiting. Her feet began to feel like lumps of ice, the chill crept up through her body. It was a quarter of six, it was six o'clock. Darkness had come, but not Steven. She kept on waiting and walking to and fro.

Cristie was right in her reconstruction of the earlier part of Steven Hazard's day. He had returned to the club after luncheon, the twin of Cristie's football ticket in his pocket. No use getting up to the stadium until after half past three.

From a comfortable chair in the reading room he watched Detectives Carr and Allen collide accidentally on the pavement outside, murmur a few words, separate and continue their vigil. They didn't worry him any. He had no doubt of his ability to shake them off at the proper time.

He looked at the clock above the doorway after he had gazed unseeingly at the early editions of the afternoon papers for a considerable stretch. One more cigarette and off to the races. He was lighting a match when the attendant's singsong voice said: "Mr. Hazard, Mr. Hazard."

Steven rose. The attendant said he was wanted on the telephone. The man pointed. "Right over there, booth five." Steven entered the booth, closed the door, lifted the receiver and said "Hello."

At the other end of the wire a voice said, "Hello Steven, having a good time, darling?"

Steven Hazard hadn't seated himself on the little stool. He was standing. He staggered. The back of his head hit the rear wall of the booth. Shock, mountainous seas of it, was sweeping down on him. He gasped for breath. Had he lost his mind? Was he going mad? He dragged himself erect, lifted the instrument in a clenched hand and said into the mouthpiece in harsh unrecognizable tones, "Who is this—who is this speaking?"

A silvery laugh, high, fluting, mannered, a laugh that it was impossible to mistake, came over the wire. It was the laugh of a woman whose lips were closed in death, a woman who was or should be lying in a satin-lined casket inside a bronze metal box under six feet of earth in a country cemetery. At the other end of the line the voice of Sara Hazard paused. There was a faint sound as though someone had opened a door. She said sharply in a whisper, "Steven, I can't talk freely from here. Listen and listen carefully..."

She began to give him detailed instructions.

Chapter Thirteen
A Scribbled Name

CRISTIE LANSING was never able afterward to recall with any clarity the last hour of waiting at the rendezvous that had been so carefully planned in advance, and at which Steven failed to arrive. She didn't leave the corner opposite the little church until almost eight o'clock. She called Steven's club from a grocery store on Hudson Street. He wasn't there. She got, somehow or other, back to Margot's penthouse, called him again three times during that interminable evening. Still no word. The people of the club didn't know where Steven was and couldn't tell her anything.

She went to bed at last, worn out with the travail of ceaseless questions, of crowding fear and bitter disappointment. No news was good news. She fell asleep to the aphorism of her childhood, woke to quiet sunshine and Sunday morning church bells. The trite old saying wasn't much, but it was all she had.

The penthouse without Margot or Euen or Johnny or Margot's constant train of visitors was huge, lonely. Its elegant spaces had a fictitious air, like an empty stage with the lights off and the actors missing.

Cristie made herself wait until half past eleven before ringing Steven's club again. The man there said that Mr. Hazard had gone out early that morning. No, he was sorry, he didn't know where Mr. Hazard could be located, didn't know when he would be back. Mr. Hazard hadn't said.

Stinging tears burned Cristie's eyelids as she fumbled her way into the living room and sat down, a small shivering figure in the corner of a huge geranium-red leather couch. Not a word from Steven. Surely, no matter what had happened, he might have let her know. She had waited so long and she had done her part. Why hadn't he done his? There must have been *some way* in which he could have gotten in touch with her.

She dashed tears from her lashes angrily. The anger was directed at herself. Steven wasn't to blame. He couldn't be. Steven loved her, he wouldn't let her suffer needlessly. There was, there must be, some reason for his silence, his absence. All she had to do was wait. There couldn't be anything really wrong or she would have heard. Her impatience was stupid. It was foolish. She was behaving like a child. But when luncheon was behind her and after she had played twelve games of solitaire and walked at least ten miles up and down the terrace and there was still no word of or from Steven, her anxiety and mounting fear got the better of her.

Another call to the club. Nothing. She called Pat Somers. Pat Somers denied all knowledge of Steven. Where else? Mary Dodd, or her niece, Kit Blaketon, might know. She rang the Dodd number and Miss Dodd offered her a measure of comfort.

"Steven? No, Miss Lansing," she said, "Steven isn't here now. But he often drops in on Sunday afternoon. Why don't you come over here and wait for him? I'm practically sure he'll be in some time before tea."

Cristie's growing panic began to recede. She flew into a dark-blue sport suit, creamy silk blouse, pulled a small blue hat down over her hair, disregarded a run in her stocking, put on lipstick crookedly, and snatched up the wrong gloves. It didn't matter. Nothing mattered, if she could only see Steven, if Steven was all right.

Her eyes searched the long softly lighted living room on the second floor of the Dodd house when the maid opened the door. It was empty except for Miss Dodd. The older woman came toward Cristie, took both Cristie's cold hands in hers and smiled down at her reassuringly.

"You look half frozen. Come and sit by the fire. There's a nasty wind out. Steven's not here yet. He'll probably arrive with the crumpets. He generally does. He has a passion for them."

Her matter-of-fact cheerfulness reassured Cristie as nothing else would have done. She was a friend of Steven's, would have known if he was in a jam. Cristie's tension relaxed. They discussed indifferent topics, the autumn, the beauty of the foliage. Mary asked about the foliage in Texas. Cristie said it was nothing to the Eastern Seaboard. Mary said the coloring was just about at its height. They ought, all of them, to get a week-end in the country, perhaps at Steven's farm, at Kokino in Dutchess County. It was a particularly lovely spot. And a little change wouldn't do Steven any harm. He wasn't looking particularly well.

"Nor," said Mary, with a penetrating glance at Cristie's pallor, "do you look well yourself, Miss Lansing, if you don't mind my saying so. New York air is all there is in New York but it isn't refreshing as a constant diet. This worry about Sara hasn't helped anybody either."

Cristie answered mechanically, her thoughts elsewhere. Why didn't Steven come? Would he never get there? Why didn't he hurry? Perhaps he wasn't coming at all. And then she heard him, speaking to the maid in the hall below, heard his footsteps on the stairs, and he was in the room.

Mary Dodd was in a low slipper chair facing the fireplace and the door. She looked up and Steven came in, stared, and frowned. The lightness of her greeting was cut off in mid-air. She said, "Steve, here's..." and stopped.

Cristie turned her head. Her worst forebodings were confirmed. Something terrible *had* happened to Steven. The blood drained away from her heart. He was different, utterly different. This was not the Steven she knew, the Steven to whom she had said good-bye with such high hopes less than two days ago. Two days? It might have been two years, the change in him was so awful. No, much more than two years, much more.

The essential bone structure, the height, the thick dark hair, were still there. But his bones had taken a twist, were tight in their sockets, had lost their elasticity. There was no light in Steven's eyes, they were deep in his head. His lean cheeks had fallen in, there were lines in them, they were hollow. His carriage, his whole bearing, intensified the impression of sudden ageing, as though he had been cleverly made-up to look as he would be with a decade added to his real age.

Cristie's cry, Mary Dodd's shocked, "Steven! What on earth is the *matter?* Where have you *been?*" produced no immediate response. Steven took off his hat and coat, folded the coat deliberately. His brown brogues were encrusted with mud and bits of briars, beggar lice and fragments of leaf were embedded in the tweed of his trouser legs.

His voice matched his appearance as he said shortly, "Nothing's the matter and I've been for a walk." Then, and not till then, he looked at Cristie. He didn't look her full in the face. His eyes rested on her chin. He said, "Hello there," dully, without a spark.

Cristie was dazed, too dazed to think. Why had Steven looked at her like that, as though he were surprised to see her, as though the sight of her was unwelcome, almost as though he actively resented her being there? She mumbled a reply and turned back to the fire to hide her face, the trembling of her lips.

Again, as she had done that morning, she took herself to task, trying frantically for equilibrium, for strength. She was being a fool. Steven couldn't talk in front of Mary Dodd, of course he couldn't no matter how well he knew her. They had agreed, hadn't they, that his love and Cristie's must be kept a secret from everyone? Steven was doing his part, she would have to do hers. Sit up straight, light a cigarette, join in the conversation, behave naturally until they were alone.

Steven had thrown himself into a chair some distance from the hearth. The entrance of the maid with the tea wagon created a diversion.

"Here, Eliza, in front of me," Mary Dodd said.

The maid went out. Cristie started when Mary spoke to her. She said brightly, "One lump. And cream, please," took the cup and sent her spoon round and round in it. The tea made a little swirl, there was a depression in the middle of it. Talk between the other two, in which she joined, talk about the coming election and Cliff Somers's chances, about Halloween and what they used to do when they were kids, about the war.

Mary knew that there was something wrong, couldn't help knowing. She kept the conversation going, kept it away from rocks. Cristie appreciated her tact, her consideration. But if she would only *go,* the girl thought wearily, if she would only leave Steven and herself alone together, just for a minute.

Presently Mary did. Attempting to replenish the pot, she found the hot-water jug empty. "One of Eliza's favorite tricks," she said. "I'll go and fill it myself. That will be quicker."

The door closed behind her. Cristie sat on, motionless, waiting for Steven to come to her, to speak. Neither of these things happened. Steven sat where he was. He didn't open his lips. A clock on the mantel ticked loudly, flatly. The silence in the room was unstirring except for that tick, tock. Cristie turned. She looked at Steven.

He wasn't looking at her. His gaze was fastened on the white Adams mantel. His face with its haunted, brown-patched eyes, was harsh, set.

"Steven," she cried, and got up out of her chair.

At her first movement, Steven rose. He walked quickly to a window and stood there looking out. Cristie stared at his back unbelievingly. Before she could speak again, his words came—level, monotonous hammer strokes with decision behind them. He said without turning, "I'm sorry, Cristie. It's all off. It's no use. It's over and done with. I'm not going to see you any more."

That was all. The floor came up to meet Cristie. The ceiling came down. There was firelight on Steven's dark bent head, reflected in a little tongue in the leather of his heel. Walls pressing close, crushing her, one of them fell open and Mary Dodd came in, water jug in hand. There were flowers on the water jug. Mary Dodd said something in a startled tone. Cristie didn't hear what it was. She only knew she had to get away through that hole in the wall that was a door.

She wasn't conscious of much after that. Between the rushes of pain and the blazing anger that consumed her she was out in the hall and was going down the stairs. At some spot before she reached the air and temporary escape, she did encounter something, something malign, the stare of a pair of green eyes from a cloud of red hair under a small hat. She thought vacantly, "That's Mary Dodd's niece, Kit Blaketon. Why does she hate me? She couldn't hate me. I didn't do anything to her." And then the coldness of the knob was in her hand and the front door was open and she was running down the steps into the October dusk.

The dusk was a cloak under which she could hide her agony, her humiliation, her trampled pride. She had wanted to help Steven and he would have none of her help. He had cast her off as though she were an impediment, a hindrance, as though he disliked, despised her. Why had he pretended all along? That was cruel, terribly, callously cruel.

When she reached it, the lights burning all over the penthouse hurt her eyes, made her feel stripped, naked. She lifted her head. No one must know, or see, or guess. She entered the living room.

Margot was there, tall, strong, ugly, and clever—and very, very smart in a severe coat and skirt that had cost an enormous sum. She seemed tired. Her abstracted gaze sharpened when she looked at Cristie. She gave her a shrewd glance, but said nothing. She had just come back from Chicago. She held square, capable hands to the fire, remarked that it was bitterly cold there. "I forgot my fur coat and thought I'd freeze. How did you get along while

I was away, Cristie? Did 'Fame' take those two full-page drawings?"

Cristie said that she hadn't finished them. Then she told Margot—there was so very much she couldn't tell, but she could tell about the visitor with the key who had mysteriously entered and left the penthouse late the previous Friday night when both she and the maid were in bed and asleep.

In the middle of the recital Margot got up and began to wander around, puffing a cigarette. She asked Cristie a half dozen sharp questions. Cristie described exactly what had happened. Margot went to a tall chromium cabinet in a corner at the far end of the room. She pulled open the top drawer. It held song records and sheet music. There was something else in it, something small that Margot took out and examined with her back turned.

She swung around toward the fire. Her face was intent, a little haggard. The freckles sprinkled over her nose and angular cheeks stood out. A pin prick of dreary wonder pierced Cristie's self-absorption. Margot was badly worried about something. Had it—the fear that was always with her, beyond and above and below everything else, stirred—had it anything to do with Sara's death? No one seemed exempt, no one.

How Sara seemed to persist, a malignant entity casting an active aura of threat into the lives she had left behind. At the hearth Margot paused. She threw the thing she was holding in her hand into the fire. There was a brief flare. Cristie was so preoccupied with the queer scene that she jumped when she heard the voice.

"Good evening, Miss Lansing. Good evening, Miss St. Vrain."

It was the Inspector. The maid had admitted McKee. He

had traversed half the length of the room without either woman seeing him. He was standing directly behind Margot. His lightning glance over her shoulder was fixed on the fire and on the object she had just thrown into it. Part of it was consumed. It was a clipping from a newspaper of the announcement of Margot's engagement to Euen Firth. The headline vanished in smoke. The whole clipping blackened. Something stood up on the blackness of the margin.

In the single fraction of a second during which it stood out boldly òn the carbonized paper, McKee got it. A name was scribbled in handwriting in the margin. The handwriting—he had examined endless specimens of it—was the handwriting of Sara Hazard.

It was Margot St. Vrain's act when she became aware of his presence that pointed up and gave significance to the scrap of paper, linking her to the dead woman. Before Margot turned, she stooped, picked up a log, and tossed it on the fire. At the impact the newspaper clipping crumpled into unrecoverable ash.

McKee made no reference to it whatever. As Margot faced him, he said pleasantly, "Sorry to intrude, Miss St. Vrain, but I've been wanting to see you for some days. If you wouldn't mind answering a few questions..."

Chapter Fourteen
THE CORPUS DELICTI

THE Scotsman stood at one of the windows of the fourth floor of his apartment in a narrow red-brick house near the corner of Forty-seventh and Lexington. The city beyond and below was black ice spattered with tiny lights that were millions of electric bulbs.

It was after eight o'clock. He was expecting Fernandez, the Chief Medical Examiner, for supper. Fernandez had arrived from his vacation that afternoon.

McKee looked northward through the darkness in the direction of Margot St. Vrain's invisible penthouse. An astute, even a bold woman. She knew her Shakespeare or its essence, had emphatically not protested too much. She hadn't pretended to like Sara Hazard, explained Sara's presence at the party from which the other woman had gone to her death, with a shrug, a gesture of her clever hands. Sara Hazard was an old schoolmate. They had known each other when they were young.

Margot had given him no fresh information as to anything germane to the crime that might have occurred at the party. Her own whereabouts? Her declaration that she was in bed and asleep when Sara Hazard's accident took place was balanced by a certain rigidity in her lean, square-shouldered, greyhound body and the important fact that the elevator to and from the penthouse was self-serviced and therefore not checkable.

When he mentioned casually that he wanted to talk to
her fiancé Euen Firth, because Euen Firth had driven Sara
home that night, adroitly concealed surprise and something remarkably like shock had flashed into Margot's cool
eyes. She had been in Chicago on business, didn't know
exactly where Euen was. He had spoken of a hunting trip
with a friend.

The clipping that she had thrown into the fire with Sara
Hazard's handwriting on it had been very effectually destroyed. There were certain inferences that could be drawn
from it. John St. Vrain had taken space in the Plymouth
Warehouse on the day after the investigation into Sara
Hazard's death began. St. Vrain could have been the fugi-
tive who had searched the Hazard cubicle. He could have
gone there to obtain the clipping. McKee turned from the
window and began to walk up and down the floor restlessly, fingering an unlighted cigarette. His brooding glance
traveled over the book shelves that lined the walls, shelves
filled with scientific treasures on every known subject.

He was aware of Hazard's abortive attempt at a getaway,
had just been in touch with the office by phone. A car
parked in front of the old church in Hudson Street had
been hired by Steven Hazard and left there at his direction. A bag in the tonneau was packed for a trip. Hazard
wasn't going away alone. Cristie Lansing had eluded her
tail at the football game. A uniformed officer patrolling
the Hudson Street beat had noticed a woman lingering in
the neighborhood of the car, a woman who answered Cristie
Lansing's description. The dead woman's husband and the
girl with whom he was in love had planned a fade-out.
Why had Hazard changed his mind at the last moment?
Why had he remained in his club? Echo answered firmly

that it was because something new had cropped up, some startling development that had halted Steven Hazard dead in his tracks. The Scotsman shook himself moodily.

Cristie Lansing, he was sure it was Cristie Lansing, wasn't the only one who had been left waiting at the church in the last few days. Pat Somers had also been given the runaround. In response to a mysterious phone call, a call they had been unable to trace and which had been delivered while he was breakfasting at the Hotel Biltmore with a national committeeman from a Rocky Mountain state, Pat Somers had taken a hasty departure—to stand at the corner opposite the Cathedral for more than an hour and a half. Nobody met him, he encountered nobody. Pat was a busy man. He hadn't gone to that spot for nothing. He had been summoned there by someone who had something of vital importance to say to him, something that couldn't be said in any of Pat's ordinary haunts. Odd, that second frustrated meeting. Perhaps the prevalence of the watching detectives had something to do with its non-result. And then again, perhaps not.

The Scotsman ran over the other cards in the kitty, Mary Dodd, her red-haired niece, the girl's fiancé, Assemblyman Somers. They were all pretty much up in the air, had their heads constantly together. He had in duty bound reported the substance of what the record had to tell concerning the death of Cliff's former girl friend and Dr. Dennison to District Attorney Dwyer. That was up to Dwyer. His business was the isolation and apprehension of Sara Hazard's killer.

Above all, the maid, Eva Prentice, occupied McKee's attention. There was no trace of her anywhere. The telephone rang. He plucked the receiver from the hook. It was Todhunter's sidekick, the burly Withers, calling. "The St.

Vrain woman is up here in the Bronx," he said. "She tried
to do a sneak but we were right on her trail. She's in an
apartment on Vyse Avenue. Todhunter's after her."

The Scotsman said, "Good. Keep in touch with me," and
hung up.

Standing in the partial shelter of an inadequate cedar
outside the Eldorado Apartments on Vyse Avenue in the
Bronx, Todhunter watched Margot St. Vrain go through
glass doors and press a button in the small white lobby. Her
back was toward him. He couldn't see what bell it was.

She turned right, went through a door and vanished.
Duplicating her movements and choosing a bell at random, Todhunter went through the same clicking door and
up a cement and iron staircase in the northern wing of the
building. He heard Margot St. Vrain mounting footsteps
above him, started to mount himself. He didn't want to get
too close, he didn't want to lose her.

The footsteps passed the second floor, went on to the third.
Silence. There were six doors opening off each main landing. Had she gone in through one of the doors on the third
floor? Kind of a shoddy layout for the elegant Miss St.
Vrain. Park Avenue was more in her line.

The mousy little man leaned against a wall and surveyed
the closed doors. His thoughts wandered. Jumbo was looking a little pale around the gills, get him some of those
new vitamin dog biscuits. A fat man wheezed upward.
Todhunter busied himself with a shoe-lace.

Fifteen minutes went by, twenty. Miss St. Vrain was
making quite a call. Was there possibly another way out
of the building? He peered anxiously into ascending gloom
and ducked like a rabbit.

Margot St. Vrain was coming down the stairs. She went past him without a glance. Withers was outside to take care of her. His job was to find out where she had been and to do a little interviewing. She must have come from either the fourth or fifth floor. Twelve apartments. The little man sighed and took up his burden.

Nothing to do but make the rounds. Apartments Four A, B, C, and D, and E were a washout. While he was questioning their occupants the fat man and two women came down in turn from the floor above. All three denied any knowledge of a Miss St. Vrain in a mink hat, mink coat, brown skirt and brown walking shoes whom the little detective kept insisting anxiously he was trying to locate on business.

The fifth floor yielded better results. A Mrs. Dennett in Apartment Five C said eagerly, "Yes, sure, I saw her. It was a swell coat, real Eastern mink with those new sleeves. She went into Apartment Five E." Mrs. Dennett pointed to a door on the opposite side of the landing.

When Todhunter thanked her and turned toward the indicated door, Mrs. Dennett stopped him. "It's no use," she said. "Mrs. Thompson lives alone. There's no one there. She went out a couple of minutes ago. She must have passed you while you were on your way up."

Todhunter's brow furrowed. After their emphatic "noes" he had given the three downcoming tenants scant attention. One woman was dark, the other was light, and the man was fat. That was all he could remember. He knocked at Mrs. Thompson's door and rang the bell, just to make sure. There was no answer. He got rid of Mrs. Dennett and a few minutes later he was entering Apartment Five E accompanied by the superintendent.

The superintendent's name was Marshall. Marshall's description was much the same as Mrs. Dennett's. Mrs. Thompson was fair, blond, youngish and rather pretty. That was all the superintendent knew. She had sublet from another tenant, taking the apartment over on the first of October. She had paid her rent in advance.

Todhunter took a quick look around. There were no clothes in the closet. The top of the dressing table was swept bare. The little detective's dismay deepened sharply. His trained eyes read the signs of what looked like a hasty flitting. The blond woman with the parcel whose face he scarcely recalled was Mrs. Thompson, to whom Margot St. Vrain had paid a visit. And Mrs. Thompson was gone.

Todhunter whistled softly. "It may be for years and it may be forever."

The superintendent unexpectedly joined in, in an excellent baritone. " 'Oh, why art thou silent thou voice of my heart?' Nice song, ain't it?" he said appreciative of his own efforts.

"Yes," the little detective murmured, "it is, very."

Fernandez stopped carving the duck at the·small table in the big studio behind the Scotsman's study as McKee dropped the phone into its cradle with an infinitesimal slam. His saturnine face was sour, set. Fernandez looked at him with surprise. The Scotsman's equanimity was difficult to disturb. The Medical Examiner helped himself to green peas. "What is it, Chris?" he asked.

McKee pushed his untouched plate away and lit a cigarette. "Margot St. Vrain called on a woman named Thompson up in the Bronx and the woman, Thompson, has vanished."

"Well—" the Medical Examiner sipped his chablis— "can't you ask the Queen of Swing where Mrs. Thompson went?"

The Scotsman said curtly, "I could if I wanted to indulge in a little waste motion. But I'm about through with useless questions. They're not getting us anywhere. "I don't like it, Fernandez. The more I see of it, the less I like it."

The concentration in his voice tightened. He kept on staring at his distorted reflection in a battered Queen Anne candlestick. "This about clinches it. Another missing woman is too much of a good thing."

"Another?" Fernandez stopped pouring wine.

"Yes. First, Sarah Hazard's maid Eva drops out of sight and now this Mrs. Thompson takes to the hills. All we know about the maid is that she used that room on East Twenty-first Street for a love nest. She and a man who gave his name to the landlady as Gray, have taken wing, are gone. There was nothing informative in the room itself except a few of Sara Hazard's cast-off clothes and . . ."

He reached behind him, opened the drawer of a small stand, took out the squat black automatic that Steven Hazard had hidden under Eva Prentice's mattress and laid it on the cloth. "—This."

Fernandez stared. McKee nodded, his mouth was stern, contracted. "There's blood and hair in the inner crevices." He tapped the automatic. "It's my belief that this gun was used to kill, not as a firearm, but as a bludgeon. But there it is. Belief. It's not good enough. I'm going to get back to basic facts and start all over again, prove every step as I go. When I crack this case I want it on toast for the D.A.'s office. What's the first thing we need in a murder trial, Fernandez?"

"All right," the Chief Medical Examiner said around a mouthful of duck. "I'll play. The corpus, naturally."

"Just so." The Scotsman struck the edge of the table lightly with a clenched fist. "And that's precisely what I'm going to get and where I want your assistance. I'm going to have Sara Hazard's body exhumed."

Chapter Fifteen
By Special Messenger

"Dwyer, I want an order for Sara Hazard's exhumation."

John Francis Dwyer stared at the man who was the head of the Manhattan Homicide Squad. The District Attorney's prominent blue eyes bulged. Morning sunlight shafting through the windows into the paneled office put a halo around his smooth, butter-colored head and his solid body, where he sat in his chair behind a massive desk.

He said with militant disgust, "So, you're still fooling around with *that* case, McKee? Yes, I got wind of it. Haven't we got enough on our hands now without your digging up a graveyard for a possible *corpus delicti?* You have nothing to go on, no real proof that there ever was a murder, nothing that'll stand up in court. I tell you you're crazy. And an order like that will create a big hullabaloo. What's the husband going to say? Besides, I understand Pat Somers has a finger in this pie."

District Attorney John Francis Dwyer was vigorous, forceful, direct and fearless in the ordinary sense of the word. Certainly he was honest according to his lights. In the radius of their orbit, these lights included a decent respect for what Dwyer termed the realities. Bashing his head against a stcne wall was no part of the program.

McKee tranquilly shielded the flame of a match that threw the planes of his lean sharply articulated face into prominence. "I want that body, Mr. District Attorney,

143

and I want it just as soon as I can get it. This *is* a case of murder. I admit I haven't got the proof I want. I'll also subscribe to another item. There's something screwy about the entire layout, a fundamentally wrong twist somewhere, that has us off on the wrong track. I'm going to find the right one. I repeat, I want Sara Hazard's body."

Dwyer remained unconvinced. He fumed. He tossed things around. He pounded on the desk. He made irate remarks about ghouls and body-snatchers, about the construction of bricks without straw, and fairy tales. McKee was firm. At the end of half an hour, the District Attorney reluctantly did what he knew in advance he ultimately would do, what he always did when the Scotsman insisted.

"Very well, McKee. I still think you're wrong, but have it your way. At your own risk, remember, at your own risk. I'll make the application, but I wash my hands of it."

That was on Monday at half past nine in the morning. On the succeeding Thursday noon the Scotsman sat at his desk considering the definite and interesting reverberations of the proposed disinterment. The application had been made before Judge Seaford in Poughkeepsie. There had been a change in Seaford's attitude after its reception. Following the normal course, the closest surviving relative, Steven Hazard had been notified of the proposed procedure. Hazard's reaction had been explosive. He had entered a violent protest against the exhumation of his wife's body.

The Scotsman's brown gaze was narrow, contemplative. All the opposition that Steven Hazard could muster wouldn't have amounted to a row of pins, if he hadn't had a friend at court. Pat Somers in New York to Judge Seaford in Poughkeepsie. McKee could have run off the talk between the politician and the judge as accurately as though he had listened in on it. A veiled threat, a gentle reminder, nothing specific or crass, and the concluding, "O.K., Pat, I'll hold the application under advisement."

In other words it had been shelved. The shelving might continue indefinitely. The Scotsman's hunger to see, to know, his need to clarify and substantiate and prove, had grown by leaps and bounds during the last seventy-two hours.

The nationwide search for the levanting maid, Eva Prentice, was quiet but thorough. It had failed to turn up so much as the glimmer of a trump. Same result on Eva's boy friend, the man with whom she had at times shared the room on East Twenty-first Street. The fellow's real name was George Loomis. Loomis was sometimes a seaman, otherwise he picked up what jobs he could find ashore. He had shipped out on a coastwise vessel as an oiler on August 26th, the day following Sara Hazard's death. The shipping office records showed that Loomis had been paid off in New York on October 11th, four days before the Scotsman's own return from Rio and five days before the arrival of the anonymous letter at Headquarters. From October 11th on there was no trace of Loomis anywhere.

Loomis could have known all about Sara Hazard from the girl friend. Cheating cheaters. He might have tried to cash in on his knowledge and, finding himself up against a tartar, might have resorted to force. The same thing held for the maid. They might have acted in collusion. If they were hiding out together or separately, the hide-outs were good ones.

Mrs. Thompson's summary disappearance perplexed him even more. Eva was admittedly a thief of both jewels and clothing. There was nothing, as far as they had been able to learn, against Mrs. Thompson. If a virtuous woman had no past, Mrs. Thompson headed the Sunday school list *cum laude*. As far as they were concerned she might have sprung into existence complete on October 1 when she sublet the furnished apartment on Vyse Avenue, an apartment that had been advertised in the papers. She had sprung out of existence with the same ease and completeness immediately following Margot St. Vrain's visit to her on that Sunday evening.

Nothing more on the night of Sara's actual death. Euen Firth, one of the last persons to see her alive, was still away on a hunting trip, locality unknown.

Too many x's with question marks after them. There was one known quantity that impeded his further absence. It was Pat Somers's determination to block the exhumation order. If Somers wanted to play it that way, a bat could be swung from the other side of the plate.

Nothing concerning the possibility of Sara Hazard's death being murder, nothing about the application for the exhumation, had appeared in the newspapers. The Scotsman had wanted it like that. It gave him leg room, space to turn around in. The time for that was over. He sighed, sat erect, picked up the phone and called Carl Randau of the *World-Telegram*.

After he had talked to Randau he rang his buzzer, sent for Todhunter and gave the little detective careful instructions. He said, "Steven Hazard owns an old farm outside Shunpike a lower Dutchess County. It's on Lake Kokino, a smallish body of water about two miles long. There's nothing else there but a hotel on the far side of the lake and a couple of other country homes. Hazard and Pat Somers have gone up to Kokino, complete with hunting gear and shotguns. Miss Dodd and her niece are joining them for Halloween. They may be there now. I believe Cliff Somers is to run up late tonight when he's finished campaigning. According to their interchanges with each other via the phone, they all want a breath of country air. I want the air weighed and measured and analyzed. I want to know everything they do, whether they contact anyone or anyone contacts them. Take as many men as you need. I' want you to pay particular attention to Steven Hazard. I've got to stay here in the city to see the FBI men from Washington. I'll join you tonight."

Todhunter said, "Yes, Inspector," and dwindled noiselessly from the room.

"Come on and help, Kit, there are millions here."

Mary Dodd was in a rough tweed skirt and a heavy sweater and had a basket over her arm. She pushed the leaves aside with her stout brogues and knelt down under the twin hickories at the northern end of the long low farmhouse perched on a shoulder of the hill overlooking Kokino.

Kit Blaketon was sitting on the rail of the veranda above and gazing off into the blue autumn haze that softened and almost hid the faint humps of the distant Catskills lying against the west. The girl shook her hair back impatiently from the shoulders of a turtle-neck crew shirt, jumped down and joined the older woman.

Shorn grass, stubbly and brown, rolled almost to the water's edge. Steven Hazard and Pat Somers were pacing a stretch of it, side by side. Pat was smoking a cigarette in short nervous puffs, Steven Hazard had an unlit pipe clenched between his teeth. His hands were thrust deep in his pockets, his shoulders drooped, his head was bent.

A late afternoon in the country, the scene was quiet, pastoral, lazy and completely normal. Pat Somers and Steven Hazard had driven up to Kokino that morning. Kit Blaketon had arrived with Mary Dodd at around four o'clock. The two cars stood in front of an old barn behind the house which backed on the narrow dirt road that circled the lake and led in from the outer world, a world that seemed very far away.

The farmhouse faced the lake. Fields stretched away in back of it tumbling up into the eastern horizon. More fields and broken patches of woodland on one side, on the other, a pine grove capped a razorback sprit of land thrusting sharply into the blue glass of the gently lapping water.

In the summer there were hammocks and deck chairs scattered here and there in the dimness of the pine grove where heavy boughs shut out the sun. At that time of the year it was lonely, deserted, its approaches choked with tindery goldenrod, masses of red sumach and giant poke. The huge pines towering above the others near the far end of the summit were a landmark for miles around. High banks descended steeply from the grove to the lake below which surrounded the long finger on three sides. The water there was deep and harbored bullheads, pickerel and bass. Judge Hazard, Steven's father, had fished there by the hour on long tranquil spring and summer days.

Pat and Steven joined the two women under the nut trees. The sun was beginning to go.

Mary Dodd rose, waving her basket triumphantly. "Taffy tonight," she said, "real taffy with real hickory nuts. You both have to help. Don't forget, it's Halloween."

Pat passed a big hand over his jaw. "I remember the potato cake my mother used to make on Halloween..."

He paused.

A boy in overalls and a jumper was coming round the corner of the house. He had ridden over from Shunpike on his bicycle. He was carrying a yellow envelope. He looked from one man to the other, said, "Mr. Hazard?"

Steven Hazard was standing a little apart. The shadows already converging on the house seemed to have concentrated themselves in his dull aloofness as he stared moodily at the distant hotel, a turreted phantom a mile or more away across the lake. He turned with a start.

"I can only deliver this personal," the boy said.

"I'll take it, lad," Steven gave the messenger a coin and the boy thanked him and departed.

There was something written across the front of the envelope. Steven Hazard glanced at it. He walked toward the steps, halted in front of them and ripped open the telegram. He read the enclosure swiftly. His back was to the others. They couldn't see his face.

Night was coming fast over the hills. A little wind had risen. It ruffled the hair on his damp forehead. His eyes were unfocused, fixed, like the eyes of a blind man. Shafted light from under a cloud touched him for an instant as he stood there holding the telegram. He looked like an animal caught in a deadfall, trying to gauge the depth of the pit into which it had fallen and exploring, with every ounce of resource, for a possible avenue of escape.

The group under the nut trees strolled toward him.

"What is it, Steve, anything important?" Pat called.

Without turning, Steven Hazard said, "No, just something from the office." His tone was gray, indifferent. He crumpled the message up and thrust it into the pocket of his plaid sport jacket.

They all went into the house. The front door closed. Lights sprang up inside. Outside, the cold purple of the twilight faded quickly into darkness. There was a chill in the air.

Todhunter huddled lower into his coat and moved nearer to the house walls.

Chapter Sixteen
A Splash in the Dark

THE MOON, nearly at the full, cast a soft silver-blue flood down over the dark night hills that cupped the two-mile stretch of gleaming water. It threw one roof of the rambling Kokino Inn into high relief, made black velvet of the other. Under the black velvet, lighted windows burned brightly. It was the night of the Kokino's Halloween dance, an annual affair attended by sportsmen, their wives and daughters, and local landowners within a radius of twenty miles. The Kokino Inn was famous for its fish and for the spontaneous gaiety of its impromptu gatherings. Quite a number of fashionable New Yorkers went there during the autumn.

The chairs and tables in the long, low, spacious dining room had been removed. Festoons of orange paper with black witches riding paper brooms draped the walls. Illuminated pumpkin heads strung across the beamed ceiling cast a mellow radiance on the men and women in evening dress dancing to the music of an excellent orchestra or sitting about at small tables against the windows.

Cristie Lansing paused on the landing of the wide staircase running down across an inner wall. The dusty rose of a dinner gown fell in long straight folds to her feet. Her smooth chestnut head was up, her eyes were more gray now than violet. There was no expression in them. They were still beautiful, tilting at an angle under the slim dark brows, but the life in them was gone.

They followed the twining figures moving in and out and up and down across the waxed floor. Margot was dancing with a tall thin man with a red mustache. Cristie's gaze lingered on her thoughtfully.

When Margot had first proposed coming up here to the Inn in her breezy offhand fashion, Cristie's initial reaction had been a violent negative. She knew Steven had a place somewhere on the lake, a place that had been in his family for years. He had spoken of it often in those far-off days when she had first come to New York before they had quarreled and separated, before his marriage to Sara. The thought of Steven or of nearness to Steven was an intolerable pain. She had to outface this pain, had to override it, push it into the background and return to at least a semblance of normal living. You did go on living, somehow or other.

It was the story in the afternoon papers that had made it more than ever necessary to preserve a façade of indifferent serenity, as though she knew nothing. Those terrible black headlines had rekindled the dark fire behind the closed door at the back of her mind. It was Margot who had called her attention to the newspaper after a late luncheon and before she had decided on this trip.

They were going to bring Sara Hazard back into existence. Cristie's nails bit into the palms of the hands hanging at her sides. They mustn't. Sure of nothing else, Cristie was sure of that, dreadfully, vehemently sure. It musn't be permitted to happen. The police were so expert, so skillful, they had ways of finding things out. Perhaps they could connect up—she made herself stop thinking as Johnny came forward eagerly from the crowd to meet her.

Johnny slipped his arm through hers. He looked very handsome in his dinner jacket with his fine head and trim shoulders. He was smiling but he seemed tired. He had skipped a benefit at which he was to have been master of ceremonies to bring Margot and herself up there to Kokino for a Halloween holiday. He not only seemed tired but there was a queer sharpness to his face.

A little pang of compunction went through Cristie. Johnny was so kind, so considerate, always looking out for her, always trying to make her comfortable. She gave him so little in return. With the pang of compunction a vagrant question presented itself unbidden. Could this trip to Kokino have been actuated by more than a desire to please Margot and herself and to get away from the city and enjoy a night's fun?

She dismissed it as Johnny circled her waist and swept her out on the floor to the tune of *All.Night Long the Glasses Tinkle*. Cristie waved to Margot as Margot went by with the red mustache. Just for a moment, in the light firmness of Johnny's expert embrace, apprehension went through Cristie. Margot didn't reply to the wave, looked at her vacantly as though she had never seen her before. Cristie's tension relaxed, light flashed into Margot's eyes and she called, "Try the punch, darling. It's real witches' brew."

That was at about half past ten. It was on toward eleven when Cristie first noticed that neither Johnny nor Margot was anywhere in evidence. Then, a few minutes later, after a rumba with a man named Carlson, Cristie saw Euen Firth.

He was standing in the middle of the long sidehall beyond the dining room. His attenuated knobby length was clad in a dark brown sack suit, he had a soft brown hat in his hand and he was staring in the direction of the side door. The door was closed.

Cristie gaped at the sight of Euen. Where had he sprung from? According to Margot he was supposed to be killing birds hundreds of miles away. Euen kept on staring at the closed side door. Thrust forward on a long thin neck his ferrety profile had a peculiar intensity to it. He didn't look at all stupid. He looked shrewd and, somehow, under that sandily inoffensive exterior, queerly excited and upset.

As she watched, he walked to the door, jerked it open and closed it behind him. Little taps of conjecture began to sound inside Cristie's brain. She excused herself quietly to her partner, took a quick look around the first floor. No Margot, no Johnny; she ran upstairs. Margot and Johnny weren't there either.

Cristie picked up a black cloak with a hood. She pulled the hood down over her hair, gathered the black folds around her. Slipping unobtrusively through the small lobby behind the game room she stepped out into the black and silver night.

It was getting on toward midnight. The half hour struck before Todhunter took his place outside the west windows of the wide-flung, many-leveled farmhouse opposite the hotel on the eastern shore of the lake. The sky was thick with piled clouds, the moon a giant jack-o'-lantern, was now hidden, now visible, behind their tumbling thunderous masses. When it went it took every vestige of light with it. All Hallow's Eve. It was a restless night, a night suited to the day and the hour, a night on which anything could happen.

The little detective was not superstitious, but the wooded

hills, the lonely stretches of lake, the absence of all sound
and motion except for the wind whistling drearily through
the trees, were beginning to have an effect upon him. That
and some sixth sense which had recorded without defining
a vague threat in the behavior of all five people he had been
watching carefully during the earlier part of the evening.

Clifford Somers had arrived at half past ten. Firelight
seeping through the drawn shades, a laugh or two, an
occasional glimpse of Steven Hazard, hadn't reassured him
any. The man was on edge and clashed as sharply against
the half-hearted merriment and the attempt to draw him
into it, as a stone in a piece of fruitcake.

From where he stood Todhunter commanded a view of
the entire front of the house. There was a man at the gates
leading to the road, another man in the meadow to the
north. Todhunter stood away from the porch wall as a
door midway along its length opened and closed and a
man's figure descended the steps and moved out onto the
dry grass strewn with fallen leaves. Gnarled apple trees
threw tangled and distorted shadows on the faintly silvered
turf. The man was Steven Hazard.

Hazard was hatless. The collar of a dark topcoat was
turned up around his ears and he carried a stick under his
arm. Fifty feet from the house, he paused near a clump of
bayberry bushes, tucked the stick under his arm tighter
and reached into the pocket of his suit.

Todhunter couldn't be certain but he was almost sure
that what Steven Hazard had taken from his pocket was a
thick roll of bills. He appeared to be counting them. He
returned them to his pocket and resumed his interrupted
stroll.

Walking more rapidly he entered a small path that

wound down the slope, rimmed the edge of the cove and struck upward into the rough hummocky ground that bordered the fringes of the long pine-clad point jutting out into the lake. Todhunter followed him as closely as possible.

There was practically no danger of his being seen. The night, the blackness in the coverts, the wind, the incessant lapping of water on shingle would have given shelter to an army of trailing detectives. The vastness of the empty hills, the stretches of marsh, the singing of the reeds, the soughing of the pines up and down, oppressed the little detective's spirits.

A crooked pear tree, misshapen against a tuft of cloud, was a crouching dwarf, knife in hand. A blasted chestnut, two-thirds of the way out on the point, toward the top of which Hazard was moving steadily, was a gallows tree rearing itself to a sudden fling of stars. The stars vanished. The moon went too. So did Steven Hazard, momentarily.

Todhunter picked him up again. Hazard was almost at the end of the tree-clad finger of land running out into the water. The path he had been traveling was only a few feet above the water line, hugged the rocky shore. On the right, the surface of the cove, cold and dark and deep, on the left the precipitous flank of the hummock overgrown with low shrubs and weeds and tangled vines. Hazard continued to go forward. The little detective stood still and rubbed his chin. Was the fellow going to walk upon the waters? An even more sinister possibility presented itself to him. There was a savage crouch to Hazard's shoulders, to his stride. It was quick and yet furtive. He very obviously didn't want to be seen, just as he obviously knew every foot of the ground.

The path, a mere thread now, wound steeply among

strewn boulders perched perilously on the tip of the point. Hazard turned, put his back to the water and scrambled up the side of the promontory above. It was crowned with a huge stand of tall pines, their trunks hidden by the sweep of tangled feathery branches. Hazard disappeared over the edge of the nearest summit.   .

The little detective crept upward in his wake. He reached a gully and paused. Confronting him, level with his eyes, was a gentle incline of slippery moss and brown, needled earth. It stretched backward roughly for some thirty feet before the trees began. Slanting moonlight fell on the great solid bank of green made by the pines and hemlocks and cedars that ran from the tip of the point toward the hidden road hundreds of yards away.

Steven Hazard had vanished again. Then, as his eyes became accustomed to the gloom, Todhunter saw him. Hazard was leaning against the massive trunk of the nearest pine. Only his legs and one hand were visible. The hand fascinated the little detective. He kept his eyes fixed on it. It held the heavy blackthorn stick which Hazard had brought out of the house with him. The stick moved slowly to and fro under those sinewy clenching fingers. The wicked knobs and stubbles on its sturdy haft gleamed a little as reflected moonlight struck them.

Todhunter peered anxiously into the depths of the wood beyond Hazard's waiting figure. Lapping of the water, soughing of the wind, louder here. Reeds rustled dryly. Was someone moving within the obscurity of that tree-clothed summit, someone who was advancing to meet the man whose grasp on the stick had tightened?

Edging forward a few inches, Todhunter tried to cleave the almost illimitable blackness under the branches with his eyes. What was hidden there? Steven Hazard had straightened. He took a step or two, stood motionless again. A twig crackled somewhere. There *was* a stir within those boundaries. Hazard had heard it. He dove forward. Todhunter reared himself in a flood of silvery light and suddenly the light was gone.

Todhunter was so intent on the scene going on in front of him that he didn't hear the creak of an oarlock, the soft beaching of the boat in the cattails below. When a hand fell on his shoulder he ducked, whirling. A voice said very quietly in his ear, "McKee, Todhunter," and the little detective relaxed—to snap back to steel wire the next moment.

Before either man could move, it happened. First the sharp snapping of dry branches some distance under the pines and then, almost simultaneously, a scream—high-pitched, thin, terrible. Overlapping it as it broke off, stopped, was the thud of a falling weight, a thud that terminated in a loud splash.

McKee was on the top of the bank and running. Todhunter followed.

Chapter Seventeen
THE THING OF GOLD

STEVEN HAZARD drew back and threw up a hand to shield his eyes from the flood of bright light that streamed out of McKee's torch. He was standing in a small clear space some fifty yards inside the grove. Behind and above and beyond Hazard the towering pines climbed up into blackness. Hazard stared at them whitely. He didn't speak. His stick was gone.

McKee wasted no more than a glance on him. He said, "Stay where you are, Mr. Hazard. Don't move."

Underbrush advanced and retreated in every direction. There were paths through it. It cloaked the edge of the steep bank running down to the water of the lake thirty feet below. The Scotsman sent his torch swinging, held it steady on one spot where a clump of laurel, its leaves twisted and bent, topped the miniature cliff.

The incline bore deadly and accurate evidence of the cause of that scream. There had been a struggle there. Someone had fallen over the brink. Twigs were broken, a small evergreen was smashed flat, moss and pine needles were gouged out and sand slid in a trickle into the black water. The trickle ceased as the Inspector watched. The water was very still.

The two men scrambled down over boulders, found a foothold. Light on the water. McKee had his coat off, ready to dive at the slightest indication of a body below that inky spread. They sent their torches in wide circles, again and again, watched and listened, straining for the slightest stir, the slightest movement. There was neither. The surface of the lake retained its flat inertia. Whatever it held in its icy black depth remained there.

The Scotsman moved at last. If a man or a woman had gone into the lake at that point it was already too late. The struggle for life was over. The water was cold and deep, and at least five minutes had elapsed since that scream. Get men, he thought. This would be a dragging job. He motioned to Todhunter and remounted the bank, taking care to keep clear of the ominous downward track.

"Well, Mr. Hazard," the Scotsman's voice was deceptively quiet, didn't match his burning eyes.

Hazard stopped opening and closing his hands and thrust them into his pockets. The night was cold. He was shivering. He said thickly, "I don't know any more about it than you do, Inspector. I was here. Yes, I was out there near the tip of the point. I heard the scream. I ran. That's all."

There was something the matter with the man's mouth. He was having trouble with it. It didn't quite close.

McKee said, "You were here. What were you doing here at this hour of the night?"

"I—" Hazard was fighting with himself. He spaced his words, bringing them forth with immense effort. "I wanted some air, came out for a stroll."

The Scotsman shook his head. "The truth, please, Mr. Hazard." Todhunter whispered to McKee and the Scotsman continued, "Of course we can search you, but it will be simpler if you'll give us an assist. What have you got in the right-hand pocket of your suit?"

There was nothing else for Hazard to do. He produced

the roll of bills. Todhunter held a torch while McKee counted. He finished, replaced the rubber band. "Always carry a thousand dollars around with you on your person?"

Hazard remained silent. McKee knew what the silence covered. A man with a thousand dollars in his pocket at a lonely spot at midnight; Hazard had received a telegram, a telegram that had shaken him, late that afternoon. There was only one conclusion possible. Hazard had had a rendezvous here, a rendezvous that had apparently ended with a scream and a heavy splash.

Whatever they were going to find in the depths of the lake below, there was no possible doubt that blackmail had cropped up again, the blackmail that had smeared itself over the case from the very beginning. First Cliff Somers, now Steven Hazard. And the maid Eva Prentice was missing and so was her boy friend, Mr. Loomis. And so too was the ambiguous Mrs. Thompson to whom Margot St. Vrain had paid a hurried and urgent visit just before Mrs. Thompson lit out.

Get on with it, McKee said to himself. A distant echo of voices came drifting through the menacing blackness of the crowding tree trunks and the crouching underbrush. He said curtly, "Come along, Mr. Hazard," and turned in the direction of the voices.

A twisting path carpeted with the slippery brown needles of uncounted seasons wound in and out through the tangled grove. It terminated in another cleared space some four or five hundred yards to the east. Ahead was the narrow dirt road that circled the lake, and to the left beyond the tree-strewn slopes, the lights of the Hazard farmhouse. Two men were standing still in the road, near the gates to the house, arms gesticulating, voices raised.

As McKee and Todhunter, with Hazard in tow, approached, the moon slid out from behind a spindrift of tumbled cloud. One of the men was Nielson, of McKee's squad. The other man was Pat Somers.

From his post by the white gates, Nielson had heard the distant scream. He had started around the curve to find Pat Somers striding hastily back along the road toward the house from the direction of the point. Nielson said as the Inspector paused beside him:

"Mr. Somers wouldn't tell me where he was coming from. He just told me to get out of the way."

McKee turned to Pat Somers. Pat was lighting a cigarette. His big face was calm in the shadow of his soft black hat. He tossed the match to the dirt of the road.

"Since when, McKee, is it a crime to take a breather and stretch your legs before going to bed?"

The Scotsman's smile was a sketched grimace. He murmured, "Odd, how many of you suddenly conceived an affection for the great outdoors." His manner was brusque. He wanted the cove beaten. He wanted whatever had fallen into the lake recovered.

Pat Somers and Steven Hazard were looking at each other. Each was asking himself an unspoken question. Steven Hazard had been on the spot or near it. Was there someone there before, someone who faded at their own approach?

McKee said, "Exactly where were you when you heard the scream, Mr. Somers?"

Pat Somers said, "I was up the road around that turn." His tone was clipped, final. His gaze supported the Scotsman's without the slightest wavering. He had no intention of going any further. Right around that curve commanded the exit from the point. Pat Somers was a quick man on his feet. He could have been there. The Scotsman swung curtly, led the way toward the house.

"I want to talk to you some more inside," he said.

As they neared the gray, clapboarded walls glimmering in transfused moonlight, the number of fresh-air fiends was augmented. This time it was by a woman. Detective Johnson, who had been patrolling the lake side of the farmhouse, had her in tow under trees over a small side porch. The woman was Mary Dodd.

Johnson said, "I heard that holler, Inspector. I took it on the run. When I got into the bushes along the shore that leads out to that point, I find this lady streaking like lightning for that pine wood. She didn't want to come back with me."

McKee's brows rose. Mary Dodd was tall and straight and very pale in a long, dark, hooded cape. The hood was down. Her head was bare. Her stockingless feet were in slippers and the folds of a nightdress showed under the cloak. She said with a concealed thread of terror in her controlled voice, "Steven, Inspector, what was it? Who screamed? What happened?"

Steven Hazard simply shook his head. Mary Dodd looked at the Scotsman. McKee said in a somber tone, "We don't know yet, Miss Dodd. Mind telling me how *you* chanced to get out here?"

Mary Dodd met his glance straightly. Her eyes were dark pools, her lips were shaking, "I—that scream—it was terrible. I had just gotten out of bed to get a drink of water when I heard it. I was half asleep. It came from the direction of the point. I threw on a wrap and ran out. And then this man caught up with me. Was anybody, did anything—?" There was a queer dread in her repeated and unfinished inquiry.

It was Pat who answered. He said reassuringly, "Don't worry, Mary, probably a pair of lovers were seeking a little seclusion. Steven must have blundered in on them and the girl got hysterical."

It didn't go down. Not with any of them. That shriek, high-pitched, terrified, chopped off in the middle, was no plaint from the lovelorn. It was the cry of a person in mortal danger. The Scotsman's long, lined face was tired as he entered the house with the others.

They went in by way of a side porch. A short corridor leafed with doors bisected the left wing. One of the doors opened. Kit Blaketon looked out at them, her red hair a tousled halo against the light of the oil lamp on a bureau behind her. She was fully clothed, wore a green sweater and a green wool skirt and saddle oxfords. Her eyes were narrow and intense in a pointed bleak face as she said coolly:

"What's all the shooting for? Oh! It's you again, Inspector."

The match she held to her cigarette was steady.

McKee bowed. He asked her dryly to tell him where she had been for the last twenty or twenty-five minutes. In front of him Mary Dodd pressed a shoulder tightly against flowered wallpaper. Pat Somers cleared his throat. Kit Blaketon said, drawing smoke deep into her lungs and exhaling it in long streams through her nostrils:

"I was in the living room, up until a few moments ago. Then I came in here—" she gestured toward the bedroom— "to get a fresh pack of cigarettes." She showed it.

"Anyone with you in the living room, Miss Blaketon?"

"No," said the girl. "Mary had gone to bed and the others

were somewhere else. I was alone, toasting some marsh-
mallows at the fire. I felt hungry."

She said she hadn't heard any scream, expressed neither
curiosity nor surprise at the information that there had
been one.

Statements for the record, the Scotsman reflected. Well,
he had them for what they were worth. Steven Hazard,
Pat Somers, Mary Dodd and Kit Blaketon were innocent
of any hand in that struggle on the point, according to
them. He had already taken in the endless doors that opened
out into the grounds from practically every room of the
rambling old farmhouse. A good many of the windows
were open too. Mary Dodd had heard that scream. Why not
her niece?

Cliff Somers was the only one not yet interviewed. They
found the Assemblyman sprawled in a deep chair in front
of a huge fire of flaming logs in the low-ceilinged living
room, at the end of several turns in the narrow corridor.
At their entrance he sat up with a start that had a flavor of
the theatrical about it. He looked first at his brother, then
at Kit Blaketon, and then at McKee. The Scotsman put the
same question to Cliff Somers that he had put to the red-
haired girl. The answer was astonishing.

Cliff Somers said, "I did hear something, Inspector, I figured it might be a hoot owl. I didn't give it much thought.
As to where I was, I was right here in this living room
where I've been practically all evening since I got here at
around ten-thirty."

"Alone?" McKee asked genially.

"Yes. Alone," Cliff Somers answered firmly and pulled
up short.

He got it, but he got it too late, the small almost inaudible gasp than ran through the huddle of people behind McKee like a flame through cornstalks. Either Cliff Somers or Kit Blaketon was lying. They couldn't both have been alone in the living room.

McKee went over the ground in detail. He took them separately and together. He measured distances and time. He consulted with the detective who had been watching the house. He studied the layout of the various rooms. At the end of two hours of intensive labor, he arrived at the conclusion that not only Cliff Somers or Kit Blaketon or both were lying, but that this might be true of the others, Mary Dodd, Steven and Pat Somers. Any one of those five people could have been out near the end of that point and could have been the agent back of that scream and that splash. They were not the only possibilities. Other angles being checked; no proof of any sort, about anything, yet.

Arrangements were being made for the dragging of the waters in the vicinity of the point, the proper implements were being assembled. The farmhouse was presumably asleep and McKee was back of the point of land when the corps of detectives searching the ground found it. Not the sinister secret that the lake might hold, but something almost equally as sinister.

Close to the spot where the broken twigs and smashed branches ran down into the water, one of his men fished the compact out from under a trampled bush. It was of gold, delicate, fragile and valuable. There were intertwined initials on the lid. The initials were "S. H."

"S" for Sara and "H" for Hazard. Light was coming up in the east. McKee stood motionless under the dark trees and stared at the golden toy for a long time.

Chapter Eighteen
A Run for It

IT WAS HALF past ten on the morning following the Halloween dance. Cristie's heart took a sickening thump when the door opened in response to Margot's "Come in" and the towering lean Inspector entered the sitting room on the second floor of the Kokino Inn.

Cristie was seated in an armchair beside the breakfast table that had just been wheeled in. Margot sat opposite. The Inspector directed himself to Margot. He said that there had been an accident on the other side of the lake the previous evening and he wanted to ask a few questions concerning their own whereabouts at the time. Cristie held her breath.

Margot dropped her allotted lump of sugar into her coffee and looked at the tall man leaning lightly against a window frame. "Go ahead, Inspector." Her hazel eyes, above square hands occupied with the breakfast tray, were direct.

McKee said, "It will save time if I tell you what we already know, Miss St. Vrain. When I arrived at Kokino last night I was informed that you and Mr. St. Vrain had slipped away from the dance downstairs and couldn't be located. In a tour of the grounds I noticed that there were a couple of rowboats missing from the collection at the dock. I took a canoe and went out on the lake. I didn't happen to run into you but you were out rowing, weren't you? You returned, I believe, shortly after midnight."

So that was where Margot and Johnny had gone. Cristie crumbled a piece of toast between her fingers and then remembered to eat a fragment of it. The crunch of the crust between her white teeth was broken by Margot's forthright, "You're quite right, Inspector. My cousin and I did go out on the lake."

"Why?" The tall man in the loose gray flannels was as incisive as Margot, consuming her coddled eggs and bacon with methodical industry.

Margot said coolly, her brows raised, "I can't see precisely how or why my movements should be of interest to a member of the New York police force.... However, I went out to meet Pat Somers. I'll tell you something else, Inspector, while we're on the subject. That was the purpose for which I came up here to Kokino. Yesterday in the city I called Pat and told him I wanted to see him. I respect Pat Somers's judgment and he knows the ropes. To be quite frank with you, Inspector, I'm becoming a little annoyed at being trailed by detectives wherever I go and by the implication that I had anything to do with the death of Sara Hazard. I'd been up here before; I didn't want to go to the Hazard place so when Pat suggested that we meet for a chat on the road below the farmhouse, I agreed."

Cristie sipped her coffee. She was afraid of the man lounging easily in the stiff chair, an unlighted cigarette between his fingers, his eyes a blank, his sardonic face expressionless. He would question everyone. Was Margot telling the truth? Would Pat Somers corroborate her story? Was that what she really had gone out for? Turning away so that her face was averted from the Scotsman's wandering gaze, Cristie listened to Margot saying categorically that the interview with Pat had not taken place, that she and her cousin,

Johnny, had never reached the opposite shore, that they had heard a cry and seen lights and people, had guessed that something was wrong and had returned forthwith to the hotel where they had gone to bed.

"What did happen, Inspector?" Margot asked.

Cristie was conscious of her own inner stiffening. She kept her eyes fastened determinedly on the chintz of the window drapes where forget-me-nots intertwined themselves with what looked like incipient cauliflowers.

McKee waved Margot's brisk inquiry aside, struck off at a tangent that brought the huddled girl in the blue sweater and blue, pleated skirt back sharply into that room above the lake.

He said, "You seem to have rather a leaning for private meetings with people at night, Miss St. Vrain. I believe you paid a visit to a Mrs. Thompson on Vyse Avenue in the Bronx last Sunday evening."

Margot laughed but her color changed. The freckles stood out on her skin. "Oh, that," she said pouring herself fresh coffee. "That's quite simple. Mrs. Thompson's the wife of an old tuba player I used to know. She was in low water financially and wanted to join her husband somewhere in the West, wanted a small loan."

"I see," the Inspector answered.

Watching him covertly, Cristie was quite sure that he saw more, much more than his words implied. Coldness seeped through her and with it a sharp jab of fear. Was Margot, along with herself and Steven and the others, caught up in the tangle of Sara, the woman who wouldn't stay dead?

Johnny came in while Margot was repeating that they hadn't touched land, didn't get out of the boat after they left the hotel. Johnny was fresh and alert in a dressing gown and slippers, his hair damp from a shower. He threw Cristie a warm smile, took a coffee cup from Margot and raised his brows at the Inspector.

"That's right," he said, reaching for a roll, "I ferried Margot out on the lake and part way across but we didn't touch land. That rumpus broke out over there and we pulled stakes."

Cristie felt the menace in the Scotsman's casual, "You're sure, both of you, that you didn't beach the boat anywhere on the opposite shore?" He placed the faintest possible emphasis on the "anywhere."

When Margot and Johnny both said no with firmness he added ruminatively, "Queer, we'll have to look for another man and woman then, because a man and a woman in a rowboat did land on that point over there some time last night. The marks of their arrival are quite plain."

Cristie repressed a troubled frown. In spite of Margot's and Johnny's reiterated assertions that they hadn't touched shore, Cristie was convinced that they had. Why were they lying? November sunlight streamed gaudily through the wide windows. It couldn't dissipate the fog banks of mounting bewilderment and the ever-increasing dread folding themselves around her, drawing closer in.

The door opened and Euen Firth's stork neck protruded around it, followed by his long gangling body clad in a rakish sports costume. He goggled at the Inspector, his large prominent eyes startled and inquiring. Margot introduced McKee and Euen said, "Oh. You're the Inspector fellow, are you, the one who's investigating Mrs. Hazard's death?"

McKee pleaded guilty and began putting Euen through

his paces. Cristie listened intently. She had thought about Euen a good deal since she had had that glimpse of him in the hall of the Inn last night. Euen agreed effusively with everything that the Scotsman produced. Yes, he had taken Mrs. Hazard home on the night she was killed in her car. Sure he had. He was a bit tight but he remembered that clearly, and how shocked he was to read of her death, the next day. He remembered seeing another woman who looked kind of like her come out of the apartment on Franklin Place. That was right. Come to think of it he had called to the woman. She walked on and he realized his mistake. No, he didn't know the woman was Mrs. Hazard's maid.

Certainly he had been away on a hunting trip. What was he doing up here? Margot was here, wasn't she, and that was a good enough reason for him to be any place. The people in the penthouse had told him that she was at Kokino. He reached the hotel at around eleven the night before, in time to see Margot and Johnny strolling down toward the water. He tried to catch them. When he didn't, he took a boat and headed in the direction he thought they had taken. But he got lost on the briny deep, you know. Bit of a muddle in the dark. Got back safe though, so it didn't matter. He had emphatically not landed on the opposite shore, didn't know anything about anything happening there and was damnably hungry. If the Inspector didn't mind—he lifted the lid of a covered dish, peered under it and rang the bell.

Cristie watched Euen straighten a dazzling tie. His rambling tale didn't jibe with the concentration in his attitude the previous evening when he had taken a sudden and hasty departure from the Inn. He hadn't been stupid or wandering or vacuous then. He had been alert and clear-headed, a shrewd, calculating man. Was that silly ass exterior a pose, a cover for something else?

At the end of another five minutes, to her unspeakable relief, the Inspector rose and reached for his soft gray hat. She had escaped; he wasn't going after her. The door closed behind him. She drew a long sigh and agreed to play a round of golf with Johnny after lunch.

Twenty minutes later the blow fell. She was alone in her own room, changing to crepe-soled shoes and a plaid sports jacket when the Scotsman followed a soft knock into the bedroom and stood looking at her. Her recoil was involuntary.

He said, smiling down at her, and his tone had a blandness which increased her inward shaking, "Don't be frightened, Miss Lansing. There's nothing to be frightened of. Or is there?"

She couldn't get away from his eyes. They were like rivets clamping her mind to his, so that he could roam around freely and examine and handle everything she kept hidden in secret corners, away from the light. She made herself tight and hard and unyielding. She admitted having left the hotel in the wake of Margot and Johnny and Euen the previous night, admitted having taken Euen's car and having driven around the lake toward the Hazard farmhouse. She denied having heard the scream. She denied having met anyone. She said that when she was almost at the Hazard house she had changed her mind and had turned around and driven back to the hotel, to find that Euen and Johnny and Margot had returned.

"Why," McKee asked, "did you go over to the Hazard house in the first place, Miss Lansing?"

Cristie pressed slim shoulders against the wall behind her. It came out before she could stop it. "Because I was afraid..."

The Inspector was scrutinizing her with interest. "Afraid, Miss Lansing?" he said gently. "Afraid of what?"

Cristie strove frantically to retrieve her blunder. She couldn't tell him the real reason, the deepest reason of all. But there were others. She turned to the dressing table, ran a comb through her hair. Facing him again, powder puff in hand, she told him about the intruder with a key who had entered Margot's apartment when she was alone there two weeks before.

The Scotsman was more than interested in this piece of information. It appeared to be new to him and he questioned her exhaustively. Relief flooded through Cristie. If she could only keep him away from that other, that first night, the night of Margot's party. She answered him as fully as she could but there was little to describe. The hall was dark. Whoever was in the living room of the penthouse that night hadn't answered her call. The living room lights had been switched off and the front door had opened and closed. That was all. She·had heard a vague sound she couldn't define. The galloping of little horses was the nearest she could get to it. She gave that to McKee with a faint smile.

"All I thought of was little horses galloping, and there certainly weren't any horses up there in the penthouse."

She watched the Scotsman file the intruder for reference. The nocturnal visitor in Margot's living room seemed important to him. He left her presently and she saw him in the gardens below. They were bare now and stripped, the borders raked clean, the leaves gone, except for an occasional oak or copper beach. The Inspector was talking to a group of men she recognized as detectives.

They were everywhere. Across the lake just visible through the autumn haze she saw the clustered boats, boats that met and collided and separated. She knew what they were doing, what was going on. She had told McKee that she hadn't heard the scream the night before, but she had heard it. The scream lay in her memory as something sharp and bright and terrible that she would never forget. They were dragging the coves over there around the point for whoever it was who had screamed. The grim fishing was so far without luck.

Johnny knocked at the door. Cristie didn't open it. She said through its thickness that she didn't want any luncheon and she couldn't go golfing because her head ached.

Johnny said, "You poor kid. I don't wonder. Take some aspirin and lie down, I'll have them send up something."

The tray was brought and removed, its contents barely touched.

The afternoon wore on. At half past three Margot and Euen and Johnny went out for a walk in the grounds. A cold wind whipped through the shrubbery, sent dead leaves scurrying. Cristie followed the slow backward and forward progress of the three of them and her feeling of stress deepened. Margot and Johnny and Euen had all been out the night before. What had they seen or heard, what were they concealing? They hadn't told the Inspector all they knew any more than she had.

Sara and Sara's death began to assume monstrous and uncontrollable proportions. It spread like a gigantic and poisonous miasma choking out all thought, all hope, everything that made life worth living.

It was the sound from across the water that touched off that snaking train of terror coiled inside of her, that was the result of long weeks, months of strain. There was a dull boom and water geysered in a huge spout, pale against trees as the depth charge of dynamite exploded in an effort to bring to the surface whatever was hidden in the depths of the lake.

Cristie stared blindly at the mud and débris and falling spray as the resolve which had been slowly crystallizing in her since last night, took definite shape. She had tried to help Steven. She had failed. Steven didn't want•her help. The tall, suave Inspector with the piercing eyes was back of that explosion on the other side of the lake. He would never rest until he got at the truth, all of it. Sooner or later he would make her talk. If she stayed. She mustn't stay.• She must get away from him, get away from everyone, now, at once, while they were up here in the country.

She started to plan. She had managed to elude watching detectives before, she could do it again. The main line of the railroad was ten miles over the hills to the east. They wouldn't look for her there, would be watching the station at Kokino. She could walk that distance with ease once she managed to shake off pursuit. It oughtn't to be difficult, if she were careful and used her wits. She was accustomed to long distances in Texas and wasn't afraid of cutting across country or of getting lost.

No one came to her room to disturb her. Dinner wasn't until seven. She hadn't a great deal of money, but she wouldn't need much and she had her check book. It was dusk when she slipped out of the hotel by a side door. There was nobody around. Three quarters of an hour later she was on the far side of the lake climbing a steep slope studded with silver birches, slender, leaning ghosts in the fading light. An open field was ahead, crowned by a grove of chestnuts and a fence. Beyond the fence lay the next valley and freedom.

She paused on a mound to look back. Below and to the right the lights of the Hazard farmhouse twinkled through the gloom, further away across the lake the sprawled hotel was a vague dark blur. Cristie turned her face to the east, gave herself a little shake and stepped out boldly on the bare, stony sheep field running upward to the top of the hill.

Just as she did so a hand seized her shoulder. The hand whirled her around. It was Steven. He had come on her unheard from behind a clump of hemlocks. He put his other hand on her other shoulder, looked down at her and said in a low voice rough with the sharpness of command:

"You little fool! Trying to make a run for it, weren't you? Don't you realize that that's the worst possible thing you could do, that it would give the whole show away?" He was savage, white, shaking as he continued, "You thought you made it. Well, you're wrong. Look down there. No, to the right."

Cristie moved her eyes. She saw the brown fedora slide behind a clump of thorn bushes. She wrenched herself free, dodged sideways and began to run back down the slope. Wind streamed past her, brambles caught at her ankles, her stockings, her skirt. She had lost all sense of direction, didn't know where she was going. The only thing she did know was that she had to put distance, a lot of it, between herself and that dreadful stranger who was Steven.

Chapter Nineteen
THE SPADE

"TODHUNTER, I have a feeling that there's something here."

The Inspector and the mousy little detective were standing in the Hazard farmyard. They were alone. Seven days had passed since that incompleted scene on the wooded point of land thrusting out into the waters of Kokino, the scene that had terminated in a scream and a splash.

It had been a time of unremitting effort on the part of more than fifty workers. Men had combed the floor of the lake in and about the point assiduously and with a complete lack of success. Eels, fish, tree stumps, rocks, débris of all sorts, had been dragged to the surface, but no body, no human throat from which that cry could have issued had uncovered itself.

The currents in the vicinity of the cove were strong and the water was deep. It was possible that the body, if there was a body, still lay far down in some bottomless hole. In any case there was nothing further to be done.

The Scotsman was dissatisfied. He repeated his statement, added, "We don't know yet what happened on that Halloween night. The secret is here someplace."

Todhunter was his ace in the hole. If there was anything here in this isolated spot in the middle of the wooded hills, Todhunter would get at it finally.

His eyes rested moodily on the big black Cadillac beyond the rickety white gateposts waiting to take him back to

New York. Poison ivy wreathed a flaming mantle of scarlet in and out of the fence pickets and spread itself over the tawny grass below. Wind whipped the leaves. The weather had turned cold. McKee looked down at the small man beside him.

He said, the backward thrust of his head taking in the silent and tenantless farmhouse, the leaden expanse of the steel-gray lake encircled by dark leafless trees, "You'll be alone here."

"Except," Todhunter murmured fondly, "for Jumbo," and gave the rope a tug. The obese animal at the end of it grunted.

McKee smiled. His smile wiped itself away. "I want you to keep your eyes open, but I also want you to watch your step. Unless I'm very much mistaken we're up against an extremely quick-witted and daring brain."

The eyes of the two men met. They understood each other. No further words were necessary. The little detective stood where he was, watching the Inspector get into the Cadillac, watching the Cadillac round the turn and disappear from sight.

As the car sped southward, McKee glanced at the hotel. Practically no guests there now; the St. Vrains, Euen Firth and Cristie Lansing had returned to New York the previous Monday. Cristie Lansing's attempt at escape—he turned that over curiously in his mind. She was a clever girl. Only extreme urgency would have driven her to that ineffectual sortie. Cristie Lansing knew something, something she hadn't so far revealed. He would go after her hard presently, when he had cleared the decks of clutter. There were a lot of odds and ends to be disposed of.

Mary Dodd, her niece, Kit Blaketon, Pat and Cliff Somers,

and Steven Hazard were also back in New York. Election day had come and gone. The good-looking, personable, intelligent young Assemblyman who had lied concerning his whereabouts close to midnight on Halloween, had been re-elected. The newspapers hadn't unearthed the link between the Somerses and the investigation into Sara Hazard's death. McKee hadn't said anything, there was nothing to say—yet. Crime and politics didn't mix well and there was, so far, no conclusive proof that the smooth, suave, young politician had had any hand in the crash that sent the Hazard car plunging down into the East River.

His mouth tightened. Pat Somers had been busy in the city pulling wires. The opposition to Sara Hazard's exhumation had strengthened, if anything, during the week that had intervened since Halloween night and that scream on the point. The Dutchess County authorities still had the application under advisement. That could go on until doomsday. Unless it came through very shortly, reflected McKee as he lit a cigarette, he would put the screws on. He would have the Commissioner and the Mayor take it straight to the Governor. The body resting in the little cemetery in the hills had to be produced.

He thought of a number of other things, of Mary Dodd and her devotion to her niece, Kit Blaketon, of Mary's fondness for Steven, of Kit Blaketon's peculiar behavior, of Margot St. Vrain's imperturbable demeanor, a state of mind with strain and sleeplessness behind it, of Johnny St. Vrain's smiling nonchalance that had iron in it, and of the playboy Firth whose vacuity covered a small but active and obstinate mentality.

McKee put his hand into his pocket and took out the gold compact that had been found in the broken bushes at the top of the slope on the point. He turned it over and over in his fingers. It had belonged to Sara Hazard, had been identified by her husband. The other articles missing after her death, the wrist watch, the emerald bracelet, the fur coat, and the clothing had not yet turned up.

The Cadillac hit the main highway, gathered speed. The Scotsman looked at his watch. He was anxious to get back to the office. They were too far out yet to use the radio telephone or he would have given orders from there. He went on ratiocinating. Nothing so far on the absent Eva Prentice or her equally absent boy friend, George Loomis, oiler. But there was a vague, a very vague line that might lead them to the strangely evaporating Mrs. Thompson. Her quick flitting from the apartment on Vyse Avenue had been too instantaneous to be a coincidence. Detectives haunting steamship lines, railroad terminals and the airports, had isolated three departures from New York during the period under scrutiny.

They had very little to go on, but they had established that three fair-haired, dark-eyed women of about the age of the elusive Mrs. Thompson had left the city on the day following Margot St. Vrain's visit to the Bronx. One woman had bought a ticket for Manila via Oakland and the China Clipper, one had flown to Mexico City, and a third had embarked on a plane for Miami with passage booked from there on a southbound Clipper.

No one of them was named Thompson—which meant nothing. Tracers had been put on all three. The Scotsman was anxious to find out whether there had been any return on any one of the women in question because he felt that back of all the surface facts, manifestations, there was movement, continued activity, that they hadn't been able to tie to anyone so far. The quest for Mrs. Thompson might be a washout. The same went for the maid Eva and the boy friend. Both had to be pursued until they were resolved.

That anonymous letter that had launched the entire investigation kept cropping up in his mind. Someone possessed of definite knowledge had sent it. Why hadn't the sender come forward? It might be because he or she was in some way involved. But if so, why had the letter been sent at all? McKee felt that if he could unriddle that he would really be getting some place. His thoughts dwelt on Todhunter. If there was anything back there in that clearing in the woods the little detective would unearth it.

Back in the leafless garden of the Hazard farmhouse the man McKee had left behind shook a finger at Jumbo and said menacingly. "Don't you ever do that again, do you hear me? Uprooting a bush—do you want to get us into trouble?"

Jumbo wagged his tail. Todhunter firmed earth with the flat of the spade around the hydrangea that the dog had torn from its moorings in pursuit of a buried stone. He shook the bush gently to see that it was securely seated and replaced the spade in the tool house on the far side of the driveway. The old gray shed was crowded with implements. The detectives' own paraphernalia lay in a heap in one corner—grappling irons, chains, nets.

Todhunter went out. He snapped the padlock into place and consulted a piece of paper he took from his pocket. The paper was spotted with grease and smelled faintly of kerosene. It had contained his lunch of cheese and crackers. There was a name written on it. The name was George Benedict.

The local storekeeper had given it to the little detective.

George Benedict was Kokino's oldest inhabitant, one of the ancients who knew everything about everything. Todhunter put the paper back in his pocket, whistled to Jumbo, got into his Ford and with the obese animal beside him, half on his lap and half on the seat, he drove up the valley to the north.

He found George Benedict in a little frame cottage beyond an old church three miles from Kokino. Benedict answered a hail from the front yard. He was a tall, extremely thin man with very black hair, a small black beard, withered pink cheeks, the eyes and voice of a ten-year-old child. Todhunter had no difficulty in making him talk.

"Bet your life I know that lake," he said. "I been fishin' in Kokino since I was old enough to spit. My daddy and my Uncle George whipped them waters before me."

The old man welcomed an audience, but Todhunter was anxious to get back to Kokino. He led the oldest inhabitant gently round to the particular part of the lake about which he wanted information.

"Yes, sir," Benedict said, "I know them pools down there round the Hazard point. Why, I caught a pickerel once near them two tall pines, it was as big as"—he sketched a miniature whale with waving arms—"and pickerel are hard to get, but I know where to look for 'em. Beeman's Cove and Hazard's Point are the best places on the lake. 'Cause why? They both lay down on a lot of rock. There's clefts in them rock walls on Hazard's Point, deep ones, and the pickerel hang around in them. You got to wheedle 'em out if you know how and you got the right bait. You take worms now—"

Benedict was still taking worms when Todhunter started his engine and drove away. The old man's surprised "Good-bye, glad you came," floated after the little detective in the chilly dimness. The light was beginning to fade fast. Todhunter drove slowly back toward the lake. As he went he talked to the dog at his side.

"Those pools around the point, Jumbo, and those rocks, fissures in the rocks. Deep cracks. The current's pretty swift. If anything did fall into that water—take you, Jumbo, or me, if we got bashed up against those rocks, we might be jammed into a crevice of them so tight that no grapples and no dynamite would ever get us out."

Jumbo wagged his tail feebly and dozed off again. It was almost dark when Todhunter ran the Ford into a field to the north of the Hazard farmhouse. McKee had told him to keep his eyes open. Night was coming. It was always possible that something might turn up. No use advertising his presence. Arrange a shakedown in the hay in the barn for himself and Jumbo. Get a few hours sleep and early in the morning make a personal investigation of the rock formation beneath the point of land and then, if necessary, get more help.

Todhunter climbed a stone wall meditatively and went through an orchard. On the right the Hazard farmhouse was dark, lightless, untenanted. On the left, the tool house loomed vaguely in the cold, wind-swept darkness. Bushes swayed, leaves rustled, and tree branches soughed up and down. There was no other noise, no indication of another human being within miles.

Todhunter leaped a foot in the air and Jumbo growled at that sudden sharp slap somewhere in front. The next moment the little detective wiped perspiration from his face and grinned sheepishly. The wind had pulled the door of the tool shed open; it had slammed it shut.

Todhunter stood still, handkerchief in hand; his eyes were suddenly bright. When he left he had locked the door of the tool shed behind him. Someone had opened it since. He walked forward. He was right. The staple that fastened the lock had been pulled out of the flimsy wood.

Todhunter eased the door from its frame gently. He stuck his torchlight inside. No human being there. He followed the light in and stood in the middle of the floor looking around. He didn't miss it at first, and then he did, and a little sharp tingle ran down his spine.

The wind cried. The lock that had been wrenched from its moorings tapped lightly on the closed door. Jumbo whimpered. Todhunter didn't move. He kept on looking at the empty space between the end of a grappling iron and a rake. Just before going out of the shed he had replaced the spade there. The spade wasn't there now, it was gone.

Chapter Twenty
WITH CLOSED EYES

THE LAST VESTIGES of color were gone from the west. Complete darkness had come. A few stars prickled the night sky. They shed very little light. The moon would be up later but that wouldn't be for some time.

Todhunter circled the Hazard farmhouse cautiously, trying windows and doors. Jumbo trotted silently at his heels. The little detective found the car on the other side of the house. It was long and low and black. He looked at it solemnly, took out a notebook and ran over a list of numbers. The car was Pat Somers's.

The house itself was tightly locked. There wasn't a glimmer of light anywhere. Todhunter tried the front door. It didn't budge. Yet someone had entered or left the house, else why was the black sedan drawn up near the front steps? Using his hands as a shield he played diminished light from a small torch over the steps. There were faint footprints on the flags at the bottom. They might be his own. He spoke to Jumbo in a whisper, made a wider cast.

A footprint that definitely wasn't his marked thick leaf mold thirty feet to the south near the entrance to a path. Todhunter struck along this path. It was not the one that he had taken in pursuit of Steven Hazard on Halloween, it was midway between the water and the dirt road and led to the inner end of the long point thrusting out into the waters of the lake.

Todhunter traversed the path carefully, ears cocked, eyes alert. He pushed branches quietly out of his way. Jumbo pattered along, now in front, now behind him. The night was featureless, filled with vague, unidentifiable shapes that were bushes and trees and rocks and hummocks thicketed with clumps of sumach and alder.

The little man wondered uneasily whether he was on the wrong track. There were no signposts, there was nothing to guide him. Then, just as he was about to give up, he came on a second footprint in the soft earth of a slope heading toward the crest of the long, pine-clad hill that topped the promontory. He kept on running a pencil of light over the ground immediately in front of him. Satiny brown needles, the exposed roots of the towering trees, blackness advanced and retreated. He tried to pierce the enveloping walls of its solidity for a sound, a movement. There was nothing but the wind and the rank tangled vegetation on either side, and the hidden water.

Jumbo pawed at a stone, abandoned it and snapped at a pine cone. He looked up into Todhunter's face. The little detective's pointing finger gestured in a circle. Jumbo obediently trotted off. He came back, looked again, started in a different direction.

Something caught at Todhunter's knee and he swung. It was only a briar. The night was pretty cold. The little detective's teeth began to chatter. The stalker and the stalked, which was which? Todhunter's torch betrayed his own whereabouts and the black walls patterned with traceries of leaf and twig kept closing in on him from every side. He waited for the bushes to move. They remained motionless until he pushed their branches aside.

His torch flicked over the point systematically from cove

to cove, moving forward toward the tip. It was a good ten minutes before he realized that Jumbo hadn't returned from his last excursion into the recesses of a small, choked grove of young pines. Todhunter whistled softly.

The whistle was light, thin, might have been the cry of a nocturnal bird. He waited. Jumbo answered. His growl was low, muted, almost inaudible. Todhunter recognized the quickness in it. Jumbo had found something.

The detective made his way in the direction from which the growl had come. The land running downward from the northern shoulder of the point was thickly treed. Underbrush crowded between the marching trees. He came on a place where a group of young poplars had edged themselves in among the evergreens.

Todhunter wriggled his way through the slim saplings. They suddenly ceased. He was in a sort of oasis, a cleared space, crowned and centered by the bare branches of an ancient sycamore, its black and white bark traveling upward to the hidden stars. Todhunter whistled again. Jumbo responded. He was not in sight, but he was near.

Todhunter frowned. He couldn't quite make it out. If Jumbo had trailed the spade stealer, the man or woman who had been the occupant of Pat Somer's car, why was there no reaction to the dog's growl? The detective didn't like it. He allowed the merest glimmer of light from his torch, in his left hand; his right was on his holster as he inched forward past the sycamore, then stood stock still.

The beam of brightness rested on Jumbo and on something else, the edge of a long narrow hole in soft earth near the rim of underbrush. Jumbo was digging. He paused to look over his shoulder, resumed his work, busily. Todhunter's startled glance took in the piles of black earth, the

leaves that had been pushed away and the length of the
excavation. That hadn't been done by the hound. The hole
was roughly six feet long by a foot and a half wide and
about two and a half feet deep. The missing spade was
thrust at a forty-five degree angle into a pile of freshly dug
soil at the end of the sinister trench hidden in that almost
impenetrable thicket.

The little detective stared down at the long dark hollow
in the middle of a pine wood in the lonely hills. Thoughts
raced through his mind, thoughts of their fruitless search
for a body in the waters of the cove, and in the swiftly moving currents of the lake surrounding the point. They hadn't
found anything. Their search was over, to all intents and
purposes. Their men had been withdrawn.

He recalled Benedict and Benedict's description of the
rock formation on which the point rested, recalled the
crevices in the rock into which a body might have been
crushed by those same swift currents. The coast was clear
of their own men. Had someone with knowledge returned
to complete the work that he himself and the Inspector had
interrupted on Halloween night?

Todhunter ran over Benedict's instructions carefully as
he stood over that ghastly hole in the ground. West of the
big rock and east of the two tall pines, the two biggest ones.
That was where the crevices were, where the fisherman, if
there was a fisherman, would be busy. Todhunter patted
Jumbo, took hold of his collar. Just before he reached the
edge of the bank sloping steeply to the water, he heard a
soft splash.

The rock Benedict had talked of was between the detective and the spot from which the splash had come. The
rock was a huge boulder with a broken and uneven face.

It offered a vantage point for observation, commanded a view of the entire point. Todhunter mounted it until the sky loomed up in front, twisted his shoulder and looked down.

At first he could see nothing, nothing but an expanse of water and the shore line broken by bushes and cattails. Then he saw the light. It was a peculiar light, faint, nebulous. It came from beneath the water, some fifteen to twenty-five feet beneath.

Todhunter gaped. The underwater light was a golden shuttle, drifting back and forth for the space of perhaps ten or fifteen seconds. The light vanished. Blackness came down.

Jumbo had climbed to the peak of the granite boulder and was nestling beside his master. The eyes of man and dog were fixed on the spot where the light had disappeared. It didn't return but something else showed. Darkness on darkness, a splash, and a figure reared itself above the surface of the lake, grasped an overhanging bough and clambered up onto the bank.

Panting breath from exhausted lungs, long, deep, tearing; a pause for rest; Todhunter strained forward. He couldn't tell whether the huddled figure on the edge of the bank was that of a man or a woman. If only whoever it was would stand up, move about so that he or she would be outlined by the slightly paler waters of the lake. Nothing of the kind happened. Instead, the person crouching on the shore dove again.

Todhunter hugged the rock with his breast. Nothing to do but wait; to move now would be premature and might be fatal. All he was sure of was that the secret visitor to the Hazard farm could swim. That meant nothing, everybody could swim these days.

The light appeared again below the surface of the clear icy water. Bubbles rose to the top. The light dwindled, went out, dropping to the bottom of the lake like a spent rocket. The figure bobbed up out of the little lapping waves, clambered back to its perch on the bank. It was holding something in its hands. Craning, Todhunter presently made out what that something was. It was a section of a thick length of hempen rope.

One end of the rope was tied to the bough of an over-hanging tree, the other was invisible, trailed downward over the edge of the bank into the lake. The figure was hauling the rope in. It required effort, there was a weight attached to it.

Wind whispering through the trees sent branches sway-ing up and down. A dog barked miles away. Todhunter laid a quick hand on Jumbo's scruff, stopping his answer-ing howl before it could come out.

Foot by foot the rope shortened. Black hills, black night sky, the ineffectual candles of the scattered stars on the pale washes of the lake, the bent figure leaned forward, shoul-ders hunched. The length of hemp kept on moving.

Todhunter eased himself down the rock and around its flank. Not more than half a dozen yards separated him from the dripping hauler and the burden that was being brought to land.

The little detective gripped his torch. He trained it on the water in front of the crouching huddle. Something broke the surface, something long—pale. Todhunter's finger moved.

A round circle of brilliance from the mouth of the flash-light rested on the thing in the water the rope was tied to.

It had a face. The face appeared, was veiled with wetness, appeared again. The eyes were closed. It was a woman who was being hauled ashore. She had been dead for some time. Fair hair trailed away from the exposed forehead. The features were bloated, unrecognizable.

Todhunter leaped forward. As he did so he collided with Jumbo and the torch was knocked from his hand. The crouching figure had sprung to its feet. Darkness enveloped the little detective and the grisly fisherman.

Chapter Twenty-One
A QUESTION OF IDENTIFICATION

THE MAN ON the bank didn't move. He had on swimming trunks and a black jersey. His hands held the rope in a tight grip. His head was bent. He raised it. Todhunter found his torch, picked it up, switched it on. The man who had gone down under the surface of the lake to bring up a dead woman was Steven Hazard.

Hazard made no attempt at flight. He remained where he was, half kneeling, half sitting as Todhunter advanced. The little detective put torchlight on the woman in the water. She wasn't a pleasant sight. The second glimpse was no more informative than the first.

All he could tell was that the woman was youngish, had fair hair and had been dead for some time. The face was hopelessly bloated. It was impossible to guess at the identity of the terrible thing looped with hemp. Todhunter put the question away from him. He had to get word to the Inspector, had to get help. Beside him Jumbo was growling softly, tail stiff, scruff bristling. Todhunter said quietly, "Nice fishing around these parts, Mr. Hazard."

Steven Hazard didn't answer. He kept on staring down at the face of the body in the water. He was wet to the skin and the night was cold. He didn't seem to feel the cold. He ran a tongue over blue lips, eased his throat out of the neck of the dripping jersey and then, at last, turned and looked at the detective. His gaze was dull, indifferent. He got stiffly to his feet, handed the rope to Todhunter without a word.

"Who is she, Mr. Hazard?" Todhunter began hauling the body in.

Steven Hazard shrugged. "How do I know? Could anyone?" His eyes were glued to the figure in the water. Dark clothing, hatless fair hair matted and tangled and intertwined with weeds; like the face the hands and the feet, without shoes, were shapeless, swollen.

Todhunter didn't persist. Hazard would have to talk later. This was neither the time nor the place. He and Hazard pulled the body carefully ashore, laid it on the bank. The detective had already made up his mind there was only one thing to do. He couldn't leave Steven Hazard alone with the dead woman, he himself had to get to a telephone. A boat would be the best, transportation would be easier that way. He asked whether there was a boat on the farm and Steven Hazard said yes.

A quarter of an hour later, the four of them, Hazard, Todhunter, Jumbo, and the long dark shape, wrapped in a blanket from the house, started across the lake through the cold wind-swept blackness of the November night. The inn on the western shore was their destination. There were lights there, and people, and telephones.

Hazard had replaced the clothes he had removed before he went into his diving act. He was at the oars. Todhunter sat facing him and the thing behind him in that improvised bier. The little detective had no occasion to use the gun in his holster. Hazard had the appearance of a man under the influence of a narcotic that had killed his brain, but had left his physical reactions untouched. His hands and arms, the powerful sinewy shoulders, moved lightly, easily, sending the boat swiftly through the water, but the man himself was lifeless, squeezed out, a shell.

Todhunter asked a number of questions. He got only one answer. Hazard said, "I heard that splash the other night. You didn't find a body. I thought there might be one. I knew about those rock crevices under the point. When you left I went down."

"Yes," Todhunter said mildly in his whispering voice, "and the spade, Mr. Hazard, and that grave on the hill, what were you going to do?"

It was useless. He might just as well not have spoken. The face of the man less than three feet away remained empty, a blank.

They reached the opposite shore. Todhunter's whistle, his shouted hello brought a Negro in hip boots and a torn sweater, and a Filipino in a white jacket running across the lawn to the dock. A half dozen other people joined the knot of men on the shore. The manager of the inn was among them.

Todhunter left the body in the manager's care, took Hazard into the hotel with him, went directly to a telephone.

At the other end of the wire McKee listened and hung up. He took the instrument out of the cradle again and called the telegraph bureau. The telegraph bureau located Dwyer at Luchow's. The District Attorney, snatched from his *wiener schnitzel* and wurzburger, said impatiently to the Scotsman, "My digestion's bad enough now, McKee. Can't a man get through a single meal in peace? What is it? What do you want?"

McKee explained what had happened at Kokino. Guesswork had resolved itself into certainty with the appearance of a second corpse. There was no longer the slightest vestige of doubt that it was murder they were investigating. The Scotsman said, "I'll take care of the body Steven Hazard fished out of the water, Dwyer. I want the other one too. I want the order for Sara Hazard's exhumation and I want it tonight."

Dwyer said, "Oh, but look here, McKee, it's after eight o'clock ..."

McKee said, "Get one of your bright young men up to Poughkeepsie. The judge will have to come through now, Pat Somers or no Pat Somers."

Assistant District Attorney Dorrens started north less than ten minutes later.

McKee was already on his way to Kokino with three carloads of men and a heavy truck.

He arrived at the inn. He viewed the sodden and disfigured body lying on trestles in the boat house. It was impossible to reach a definite conclusion of any sort about it. The water had done its work too well, the water and the rocks and the swift currents. The local doctor who had been called refused to make even a guess as to how long the dead woman had been in the lake. He hemmed and hawed, and polished his glasses.

The Scotsman didn't press him, Fernandez would take care of that later. All that was perceptible to the casual eye was that the dead woman was young, had been slender, and had blond hair and brown eyes, a 'description that would fit roughly some half million people.

McKee talked to the state police. He talked to Hazard, with no better success than Todhunter had had. He went over to the point, returned to the inn. The exhumation order came through shortly after midnight. The Scotsman was prepared for it. Men had been waiting in the cemetery with the necessary equipment. It was on toward three o'clock when McKee was informed that the actual disin- terment was about to begin.

The little cemetery lay on the slope of a hill to the north of the village. The dim bulk of an old white colonial church rose beyond tall elms that ringed the graveyard on three sides. White stones glimmered palely through the dark- ness, some of them at a slant. A small faded American flag hung over a neighboring plot. There was no wind; dried wreaths, clumps of fading flowers, were still in the frosty and unstirring black night.

Grotesque shadows shot out from the steel-blue flood of brilliance cast down by the elevated searchlights. The head- stone had been removed. It was propped against a marble angel on the left. A stretch of dry turf, an oblong of it, had already been dug out. Sandy soil extended flatly. The inscription of the tombstone leaning against the angel read:

"SARA HAZARD, wife of STEVEN HAZARD. Born, March 1, 1912. Died August 25, 1940. *Requiescat in pace.*"

Rest in peace. More turf was lifted off. McKee signaled to the waiting men. The spades flew.

Todhunter stood beside the Inspector during the prog- ress of that swift and accurate performance. Dig and throw, dig and throw, the pile of excavated earth grew. The oblong hole deepened. The Scotsman didn't talk. He made no mention of the other body that had been taken from the icy waters of the lake lying cupped in a hollow far below, nor did he refer to the missing maid, Eva Pren- tice, or the vanished Mrs. Thompson, both of whom had blond hair and brown eyes.

The work was almost over. Shovels scraped against metal. A little more depth at the sides and ends; the last crumbs of earth were brushed away. Relentless radiance beat down on the bronze box that enclosed Sara Hazard's coffin. Two men descended nimbly into the cavernous trench. Ropes went slithering down. Shovel, shovel again, push, tilt, draw. More ropes were added, the men clambered up out of the open grave. Twelve pairs of hands seized the ropes. Slowly, very slowly, taking care to avoid an accident, the long bronze box began to rise.

A truck had been backed to the iron railings that enclosed the Hazard plot. The bronze box was lifted into it. McKee got into the Cadillac. The procession of cars drove round the lake. The other body, the one Steven Hazard had so conveniently produced for them, was laid beside the bronze casket in the truck. Hazard was brought out of the inn, put into one of the police cars in Lieutenant Sheerer's charge. McKee had nothing more to say to Hazard at the moment. That was for later.

The funeral cortège started south over the hills toward the main highway. The light was coming now, a vast translucent purple heralding another day. The two women, coffined and uncoffined, rode side by side under the tarpaulin. Beyond the village McKee signaled to the man at the wheel, and the Cadillac cut around the truck and was off. The Scotsman was in a hurry.

Mile after mile of woods interspersed with fields and little towns fled by. The light grew. The Scotsman sat silent in a corner of the Cadillac. Todhunter watched him from the other corner. The Inspector's long dark face was inscrutable. The little detective sensed the fire of impatience under its immobility.

Full day now; the sun was coming up in the east. As they

crossed the city line, McKee's arm shot out. They were within reaching distance now. He picked up the radio telephone and spoke into the mouthpiece.

When the Chief Medical Examiner answered sleepily, the Scotsman said, "Fernandez? McKee. Rise up, Father William. I've got work for you to do. Two dead women. Both bodies were in water for a considerable length of time after death. The features are a washout, no earthly good. If possible, I want the two women recreated. I want you to try a Hoffman."

Chapter Twenty-Two
A Cloud of Blackness

McKee's call to the Chief Medical Examiner was made on Friday morning at 7:47 a.m. It was on the afternoon of the following day, Saturday, at twenty minutes after one that Cristie Lansing received the telephone call from Pat Somers. Pat simply asked her to come to his house on East Eighty-first Street as quickly as possible. He didn't say why and Cristie didn't ask. She agreed listlessly. All her reactions were listless during those days.

When she got to the old-fashioned brownstone house on the East Side, she found Margot, Johnny and Euen seated in Pat's office together with Mary Dodd and her niece Kit Blaketon and Clifford Somers. Pat's opening announcement wiped out her surprise at finding them all there together, wiped out everything. Steven had been arrested and taken to Headquarters. She heard Pat saying hazily and from a distance, "We were in the middle of lunch at Steve's club when a couple of detectives walked in. I wanted to get a lawyer but Steve wouldn't let me. He said he was going to see it through on his own. I think he's foolish. He's down there with McKee now. God knows what's going to happen."

The grayness around Cristie thickened. She could see the others through it, but not very well. They were all sitting stiffly erect and their faces were all white and strained. She wondered a little about that. Why should they care?

It didn't matter to them, they didn't love Steven; not the way she did. Her heart cried out at the thought of him, in the middle of a circle of ruthless men, surrounded by them, being questioned hour after hour, perhaps even behind bars.

She stilled the tumult beating back and forth within her breast, forced herself into the present. Pat Somers, she told herself desperately, was a friend of Steven's. Pat would save him if anyone could. She drew breath in and out of a dry throat, clasped her hands tightly together in her lap and examined Pat with new eyes. Had she been wrong all the time? Should she have spoken? Was her silence a mistake? The possibility of error was there. She had to make a decision. It couldn't go on like this much longer.

Pat tapped a pencil on the desk at which he was seated. He said in a somber voice, looking slowly around the room, "Steven Hazard's father was a good friend to me and Steve's in a bad jam. I asked you to come here for a definite purpose. I know and you know that we've all been more or less forced to keep certain things from the police. That was all right. But the time has arrived for us to come clean, at least among ourselves, to clear the decks and throw in everything we know in the hope that out of our combined knowledge we may be able to find something that will save Steven."

Cristie's eyes clung to Pat. He was forceful, he seemed sincere. The rush of hope his words sent surging through her died. They were all staring at Pat but no one spoke. Euen coughed and shuffled his feet. Neither Margot nor Johnny said anything. Kit Blaketon recrossed her knees, examined a lacquered nail. Cliff Somers smoothed down a crisp wave of hair impatiently. Mary Dodd's gaze was as eager as Cristie's. But Miss Dodd was troubled about something. She looked older, thinner and there was a peculiar rigidity to her.

Silence and more silence. Cristie writhed inwardly. Wasn't anyone going to do anything, to give him any help? She tried to swallow and couldn't. She would have to speak. If she did, perhaps someone else would come through with something. She would have to open that door at the back of her mind, make the terrible knowledge behind it public.

But did she dare? She went over the distant August night again, painfully, laboriously, with anguish. Her body was in the room with those others, who had all played a part in the drama of Sara Hazard's death, but she was out of the room. Her brain groped blindly in half a dozen different directions, weighing, assembling, discarding. Heat was going through her in waves, but her fingers were ice cold.

At the other end of a reversed telescope the tiny figure of Kit Blaketon sat with green eyes fastened on the floor. Cristie's gaze swept past her, went beyond the confines of the house in a desperate racking voyage. She relived those terrible minutes on Franklin Place during the early hours of August 25th, her approach, her flight. The awful knowledge that had come to her then, the knowledge that she had refused fully ever to face, that she had hidden away and battened down because she might be wrong, now had to be produced.

It was as she sat there, shoulder blades pressed hard against the back of the Windsor chair, that the truth came home to her—not the whole truth, but a flash of it that changed the universe. She had been mistaken all the time. What she thought she had seen, wasn't really what she had seen at all. She had been stupidly, criminally blind, she had been betrayed by her own cowardice, her own fear.

She didn't know where the revelation had come from except that it was from someone or something within the room. It didn't matter. She didn't stop to do any analyzing. Exultation flooded through her. She wanted to leap to her feet, to laugh, to cry the truth aloud.

She blinked vagueness from her lashes, looked around. The little office came back into view, the office and the people in it. She looked at Pat at the desk. She moistened her lips with the tip of her tongue, tried to keep her tone level, tried to keep breathlessness out of it, and said, "I know something. I was there, on Franklin Place on the night Sara Hazard was killed. I was on the corner across the street from Steven's apartment. I saw Sara Hazard come out and go around the corner and get into the car. I saw someone else join her. I ..."

Cristie paused. She stared fixedly at the blue-glass ash tray in front of Pat. It was full of cigarette butts and ashes and yellow matches. Water ran somewhere. Margot shifted in her chair and taffeta rustled. A window curtain blew in and out. Cristie almost had it, the detail that had slashed its way through the fumbling darkness of her mind a few minutes earlier. The detail had escaped her, was gone. She continued slowly, aloud, "There was something about the person who got into the car with Sara ..."

It was Johnny who interrupted her. He was composed enough, but there was a hard edge to his voice. He said, "Cristie, my dear, you're getting rather involved. Who was it you saw, if you saw anyone? Don't keep us in suspense."

"Exciting, what?" Euen Firth's gloved hands folded themselves over the top of the stick on which he leaned. He guffawed nervously.

Cristie pushed hair back from her forehead. "I'll begin from the beginning. On the night of Margot's party I left the penthouse and went up to Franklin Place. I was worried about Steven. Sara had refused to give him a divorce. I knew how he felt and I was afraid that something was going to happen. I wanted to see him again, talk to him before he and Sara met.

"I didn't get as far as the apartment. While I was on the corner across the street I saw Sara come out and go around the corner and get into the car which was parked a little way down the hill. The car was opposite me, on the other side of Franklin Place. Sara was in it when the other person approached and got in beside her. I didn't see where the other person came from. It was pretty dark. I did see the car start down the hill and then, after it had gathered speed, I saw someone jump off the running board and disappear into the shadows of the side street. The car was running down the hill, out of control. I heard the crash. I ran down and joined the crowd. I couldn't tell who the person who had been with Sara was. It was very late and there were no stars and the night was very black. But I thought, that's what made me do so many goofy things since, I thought . . ."

It was Margot who said with quiet sympathy, "You poor kid. Of course, you thought it was Steven Hazard."

Clifford Somers asked carelessly, "And it wasn't Steven?"

Cristie turned to him. "No, it wasn't Steven," she said swiftly. "I understand that now. But I thought all along it was. That's why I dodged the police at the football game, why I was going to marry Steven, whether he liked it or not, so that the police couldn't make me talk, couldn't put me on the witness stand against him. That's what made me try to get away up at Kokino after the night that woman screamed out on the point. I thought all the time that it was Steven who had killed Sara and now I know it wasn't Steven!"

Pat was the one who broke the pause that followed her rush of words, an odd, still small pause. He said thoughtfully, "You're quite sure that the person who joined Sara after she went round the corner that night wasn't Steven, Miss Lansing?"

Cristie said firmly, "I'm quite sure. I'm absolutely positive. There was something"—she studied the pattern of the rug absently, a vertical line between her delicate dark brows, tried to concentrate—"there was something definite after I came in here, something ..." She shook her head, threw back her shoulders impatiently. "There, I almost had it. Now it's gone. But it will come back. It's only a small detail, yet it's conclusive. If I could only get hold of it. Wait ..." She put a finger to her lips, but the elusive memory refused to return.

Sitting motionless, absorbed in the effort at recollection, Cristie felt suddenly cold. There was an icy quality, a chill suspended breath in the waiting quietude. It penetrated her self-absorption. She returned sharply to consciousness. From whom or what had that menacing coldness come? The sensation was as strong as though she had been thrust into a bitter draft. There was no indication in any one of the people seated around the office of the source of that bone-piercing chill. It was true that they all looked strained and tired. There was nothing more than that. In spite of her new-found reassurance, her terrific relief, her joy, her uneasiness remained.

She got up out of her chair. "I'm going down there to Police Headquarters now. I'm going to tell the Inspector the truth."

Margot and Johnny smiled at her. Euen's glance was admiring.

Pat Somers said, "Wait a minute, Miss Lansing."

Clifford Somers and Kit Blaketon were looking at each other.

Mary Dodd said wearily, "But Pat, she's right. Something had to be done."

Pat said, "I realize that, Mary. But the situation has got to be properly handled. Miss Lansing thinks she knows something that will clear Steven. Splendid." He turned to Cristie. "Will you leave this to me?"

Cristie hesitated, but Pat was so big, so solid, so competent and a few hours couldn't possibly matter. She nodded.

"Very well," Pat said. "Go home, my dear, and sit tight and wait there until you hear from me."

That was the way it was left. They all separated. Margot had to go down to her office and Johnny was due at the studio. Cristie was glad to be alone. She walked back to the penthouse.

The afternoon was gray with an overhanging sky and a wind that had a bite to it. Cristie disregarded the grayness. She continued to push aside the faint uneasiness that still lingered within her. Nothing mattered now except that in a few hours Steven would be free. The person she had seen leap from the running board of Sara's car was the person who had killed Sara, and that person was not Steven.

There was no answer to her ring at the door of the penthouse. The maid must be out marketing. Cristie used her key. She took off her hat and coat, wandered into the living room and walked up and down after a glance at the clock. It was a quarter of four. Not quite an hour since she had left Pat Somers's; she mustn't be impatient.

She went into her bedroom, sat down at her drawing board and tried to do a sketch, but work was impossible. She got a glass of milk and a cracker in the kitchen. The minutes dragged. She took herself firmly in hand. She was only making matters worse, prolonging the interval of waiting by thinking about the passage of time.

She returned to the living room, took a novel by Trollope from the bookcase and settled herself determinedly in a deep wing chair in a corner. The chair faced the west window. It was growing darker out. The door was dim. She switched on the lamp at her elbow, opened the thick squat red volume.

Outside the city began to fade. Margot's chromium clock struck a quarter past four and then half past. Cristie refused to let herself look at the clock, kept her eyes fastened on the type resolutely. It was a few minutes after the second chime when she thought she heard the front door closing, but when she called there was no answer. She went on reading.

And then without any warning or any noise of any kind, she smelled that sweet nauseating odor, the odor she associated with having her appendix out.

Before she could move or turn or do anything, a hand reached down over the back of the wing chair and clamped itself tightly over the mouth she opened wildly in an attempt to scream. The effort was a failure. The scream didn't come out. She struggled desperately to free herself from that enveloping grip. She couldn't. Her head went back against the cushions of the chair, a cloth was pressed over her nostrils, stopped her breath. Blackness, a great cloud of it, soft, yielding, settled down over her.

Chapter Twenty-Three
Two Heads

Steven Hazard rearranged himself against the leather cushions of a chair in the outer office of the Police Commissioner's rooms. He was very tired. The Commissioner himself, District Attorney Dwyer, the Inspector and two stenographers were inside. Hazard had been called and recalled half a dozen times since one o'clock. It was twenty minutes after three in the afternoon. Fatigue dulled his wits, weighted his eyes. If they'd only let him alone, let him sleep. He felt as though he could sleep for a solid month. He blinked at the closed door in front of him.

Beyond it, the pile of reports on the Commissioner's desk kept growing. Relays of messages for the Inspector continued to arrive. McKee digested the latest bulletin, looked up from it, his expression smug, satisfied. He started to pace the floor, went on pacing as he talked.

"There it is, Commissioner. You can take a look at it for yourself. I felt all the time that the St. Vrains had a heavy stake in this somewhere. Now we know."

At the window Dwyer said hastily, "What? What?" and stopped rumpling his short butter-colored hair. McKee condensed for him. He sketched briefly the search for the elusive Mrs. Thompson who had faded from the picture immediately following Margot St. Vrain's visit to the flat on Vyse Avenue in the Bronx. Mrs. Thompson was the woman who had booked passage in New York the next day on the Clipper for Haiti. Mrs. Thompson hadn't arrived in Haiti. She was still among the missing.

But the Haitian police had gotten hold of Mr. Thompson, the woman's husband. Only he wasn't. Dwyer scowled. "Can't you make up your mind, McKee?" The Scotsman smiled. Charles Thompson was a sort of master of ceremonies at the Hotel San Sebastian in Port au Prince and under threat of having his head torn from his shoulders and consumed before his eyes, Mr. Thompson had not only talked, he had been verbose.

Charles Thompson had once been a teacher of French at Miss Brandon's exclusive school for girls in New York. It was at Miss Brandon's that he met and married Margot St. Vrain, at that time a pupil instructor in the same school. They had kept the marriage to themselves for fear of losing their respective jobs. Several years later Thompson had taken passage on the ill-fated *Kestril* which went down in the Caribbean with a terrific loss of life. Thompson's name was erroneously included in the list of the dead.

He was merely injured. He admitted that when he left the hospital he failed to correct the error, let Margot St. Vrain continue to think he was no more. Their marriage had not been a happy one and a tropical tramp's free and easy life appealed to Thompson much more than being the husband of a rather severe taskmistress. So much for the past. Thompson had become strangely silent when questioned as to the woman who had been using the name of Mrs. Charles Thompson in New York. As far as Sara Hazard was concerned, he admitted that he had run into Sara Hazard, formerly a pupil at Miss Brandon's, when she was in Haiti on a cruise a year earlier.

Dwyer and the Commissioner stared. McKee nodded.

He said, "Undoubtedly Sara Hazard attempted to black-mail Margot St. Vrain with the information about Thompson she had picked up on that cruise. It wasn't any good until she read the announcement of Miss St. Vrain's engagement to Euen Firth. I imagine that Miss St. Vrain, or Mrs. Thompson if you will, was ignorant of the fact that she had a live husband when she contracted the engagement. Then Sara Hazard came along."

"Why," Dwyer demanded, "didn't that swing woman just get a divorce and tell Sara Hazard to chase herself?"

"For two reasons," McKee answered. "Margot St. Vrain didn't know Thompson was alive until Sara Hazard put the heat on her and, after that, well, I've met Euen's father and mother. Stiff old couple. They wouldn't look kindly on a divorce. Margot St. Vrain knew that. So did Euen and so did Johnny St. Vrain, Margot's cousin.

"Sara Hazard clipped a notice of Margot St. Vrain's engagement out of the paper. The name Mrs. Thompson was scribbled in the margin in Sara Hazard's handwriting. The clipping was in Sara Hazard's desk when she died. As soon as we appeared on the scene, Johnny St. Vrain, anxious to protect his cousin, who, incidentally, would be the wife of an extremely rich man, went to the Plymouth ware-house, removed the clipping from Sara Hazard's effects and gave it to Margot. Margot St. Vrain destroyed it while I was in the penthouse. I was no sooner gone than she made a beeline for that Vyse Avenue Apartment. Whether she paid over some cash to the mysterious Mrs. Thompson we can't find out. I think she did."

"Let me understand you, McKee," the Commissioner interrupted. "Are you accusing these three people, Margot St. Vrain, her cousin and her fiancé separately or together?"

The Scotsman said, "I'm not accusing any one of them directly. I am saying that they had a strong motive for murder and also that they had the opportunity to commit it. The woman whom Steven Hazard identified as his wife, the woman who was drowned in the Hazard car on the morning of August the 25th, was killed directly after Margot St. Vrain's party at the penthouse. Neither Margot, her cousin Johnny, nor Euen Firth has an alibi for the period in question. Not only that, but their conduct since has been suspicious. All three of them could have been out on the point up there at Lake Kokino when a woman screamed some five days before Steven Hazard fished that second body out of the water.

"The St. Vrains and Firth had company. Pat Somers was close to the point that night."

Dwyer flinched a little at the mention of Pat. McKee continued, his eyes cold, "Pat Somers had an ample reason for killing. His brother was being blackmailed. Pat's been doing a lot of queer things; the same goes for Mr. Clifford Somers. Not only his political career but his marriage was at stake.

"Kit Blaketon had motive for murder, the best there is, jealousy. She didn't know until that record was played in Pat's office what was really going on. And either she or Cliff or both lied about where they were during the scene that took place on that point on Halloween night. Mary Dodd had a motive for murder. She's devoted to her niece and also she's fond of Steven Hazard. What's more, Miss Dodd was between the house and the point when she was discovered after that scream and that splash."

The Commissioner said, "As I remember, she said that she was at home and in bed the night Sara Hazard's car crashed."

McKee stroked a long upper lip. "Yes, that's what she said. Kit Blaketon said she was in bed, too. But like all the others"—he shrugged—"no proof."

Dwyer's impatience was growing by leaps and bounds. He swung on the Scotsman. "For God's sake, McKee, get down to the meat of it. Who in hell is the woman Steven Hazard fished up out of Kokino Lake?"

McKee was standing at a window. His glance rested on another window in the Police Academy across the street, on a row of windows on one of the upper floors. Fernandez was busy behind those windows. He said, "As soon as the Medical Examiner has completed his work I'll be able to tell you, but not until then."

Dwyer snorted. "There are too damn many intangibles in this whole case. What about the maid, Eva Prentice? What about her boy friend, Loomis?"

McKee blew smoke thoughtfully. "I have hopes of getting my hands on the boy friend shortly. As for the missing Eva, I haven't the slightest idea where she is. We do know this much. Like mistress, like maid—Eva followed in her employer's footsteps. I'm convinced that whatever damaging information Sara Hazard had in her possession the maid also had. She shared a room with the boy friend. Neither of them has been back there. They've both dropped out of sight."

"All right," Dwyer said. "A room, that's where the gun was found, wasn't it? What about the gun?"

McKee said, "Suppose we have Hazard in again and get him to tell us."

Steven Hazard's eyesockets were leaden as he faced the three men in a chair placed to the left of the Commissioner's desk. Hazard's fatigue, mental and physical, was obvious. He remained firm under the District Attorney's onslaught.

On the night the gray convertible went into the river it was true that he had been wandering around the streets. He admitted having gone to the warehouse in search of the gun.

McKee said, "But you didn't find it there, did you? And you trailed Johnny St. Vrain away from the warehouse because you thought he might have it. That didn't get you any place. But you did find the gun in Eva Prentice's room on East Twenty-first Street. You not only found it, you wiped fingerprints from it. How did you know that gun was there in the maid's room?"

Hazard said tonelessly, "I got a letter telling me exactly where the gun was. A door key was enclosed in the letter."

"Pay anything for it, Mr. Hazard?" Dwyer wanted to know.

"Yes," Steven Hazard said, "I paid a thousand dollars, a thousand dollars I was instructed to send in a plain envelope to Arthur Brown, general delivery here in New York."

The Commissioner pressed a button on his desk.

McKee said, "Mr. Hazard, that wasn't the only message you received. There were two or three others. You got a message telling you not to go through with that trip south with Cristie Lansing on the day she evaded our man at the football game. You got a message to be at a certain spot out on that point up at Kokino at a certain time and to bring another thousand with you. Those instructions were given to you in a telegram that was delivered after you arrived at Kokino on the afternoon of the 31st of October.

Who sent those messages?"

Hazard simply looked at him. The force of the Scotsman's bright brown gaze didn't make a dent in him.

McKee went on quietly, "We know what you've been doing, Mr. Hazard. You've been trying to shield Cristie Lansing all the time. The person who sent you those messages threatened to name Cristie Lansing as your wife's murderer, isn't that so? You have an idea who the sender of those notes was. You thought that person was killed on Halloween night when you heard that scream and that splash. That's why, when our search for a body failed, you investigated the crevices yourself. You wanted to make sure, wanted to hide for all time the person, or any clue to the person, who was a threat to Cristie Lansing."

The early dusk of late autumn had entered the room. The Commissioner made no effort to turn on the lights. He was gazing at Hazard and from Hazard to the Scotsman. McKee had something up his sleeve. He went on talking to the engineer.

"In any case, Mr. Hazard, you would have failed. You would have failed because only the Hoffman test, a highly specialized operation, could hope to reveal the truth."

Steven Hazard didn't speak. Dwyer did. The exhumation of Sara Hazard and the sudden projection of another body, the body of an unnamed woman who had been drowned, had him badly worried. McKee's cryptic remarks of tests and processes were all very annoying to him. The District Attorney burst into angry speech. "Hoffman, Hoffman! Who the hell is Hoffman and what's Hoffman got to do with this investigation?"

McKee turned to Dwyer. He said softly, smoothly in the twilight sifting through the window, "Professor von

Hoffman was an eminent European medico-legal expert. Unfortunately he's dead now but the experiment to which I have reference is still in use. Would you like a description of it?"

He didn't wait for Dwyer's grunt. "I'll give it to you in detail, as it happens to be extremely important. When a corpse cannot be identified with certainty by the clothing or other general characteristics, the brain is removed and several deep cuts are made in the back and sides of the head. In twelve hours' time the green coloring of the skin disappears or blanches and the swelling diminishes. The top of the skull is then replaced and the skin sewn up again. After that the head is plunged into a concentrated solution of alcohol. Twelve hours later, with luck, the face will have assumed its normal condition and will present the appearance of a corpse newly embalmed. That's what Fernandez has been busy about since yesterday morning."

McKee had timed it right, but then he had seen shadows in the lab across the street. He had scarcely finished speaking when the door opened and Fernandez, the dark, elegant Medical Examiner entered the room. Fernandez was followed by two white-coated laboratory attendants. Each of them carried a box. The boxes were approximately a foot and a half square. The experiment was over. At Fernandez's direction the assistants placed the twin boxes on a long table against the wall beyond the Commissioner's desk.

McKee looked at the Medical Examiner.

Fernandez said, "Sure enough, Inspector."

The sudden silence was taut. The Scotsman was moving toward the long table when the telephone rang. The call was for Steven Hazard. Carey looked at McKee. McKee nodded. The Commissioner pushed the instrument toward

Steven Hazard. Hazard took it. He said, "Hello," and then all expression was wiped from his face.

A woman's voice repeated itself quite clearly in the stillness of the dusk-filled office, a woman's silvery laugh rang. "Hello, Steven, darling..."

McKee's hand shot out. He took the receiver from Hazard, clamped it to his ear. There was a pause at the other end of the wire and what seemed like a faint gasp. Then there was a click. Just before the click came there was another sound. It spun down an alley in the depths of the Scotsman's mind, rocketed into its appointed slot. He knew then who the murderer was. He turned to Steven Hazard.

Hazard was ashen. He was shaking like a man in the grip of a malarial chill. He looked at McKee. He said slowly, "Yes, Inspector, you were right. That was my wife."

The Commissioner and Dwyer stared at the engineer seated there in the chair in front of them as though he had gone mad. His wife—but his wife was dead. McKee wasn't looking at Hazard at all. He was at the table on which the two boxes rested. His fingers moved over the catches on the box labeled "Body Exhumed From Hazard Grave, Kokino." He lifted the lid. The sides automatically released themselves, fell to the table. The Scotsman's tall figure hid what the box contained from view. He said over his shoulder, "No, Mr. Hazard, that wasn't your wife on the other end of the telephone just now. This is." He stepped aside.

Light from the tall windows fell slantwise on the exhibit on the table. It was small and exquisite and vivid and terrible. Alabaster cheeks and chin and brow. The head was mounted on a pedestal. Golden hair, long narrow white face, the eyes were closed. Sara Hazard gazed sightlessly at nothing in the petrified quiet of the Commissioner's shadowy office.

It was Sara Hazard whose body had been plunged down the hill into the river on that August night. It was Sara Hazard whom Steven had identified at the morgue on the 16th of September.

Sara Hazard had been dead all the time. There was no longer a living Sara. Someone had skillfully made use of the dead woman, reproducing her voice, making her walk and talk when it became necessary to do so.

Dwyer was knocked ipsy-endways. He wiped sweat from his forehead, croaked hoarsely, "The maid! Eva Prentice. Eva Prentice has been impersonating Sara Hazard. She ..."

McKee was at the second box. He said, "I don't think so, Mr. District Attorney." The box opened. The head belonging to the body that Steven Hazard had fished up out of the lake at Kokino was revealed.

It was the head of Eva Prentice, the Hazard's missing maid.

A gasp of revulsion, nausea, from Steven Hazard. He covered his face with his hands. Dwyer and the Commissioner continued to stare wryly at the grisly exhibition. They were too startled for speech. The Scotsman didn't say anything. He was on the phone, the inside phone this time. He called the telegraph bureau.

The operator at the long green table in the golden bowl at the top of the great gray building consulted a list of names. They were the names of detectives tailing the people under observation in the Hazard murder case. The operator began giving McKee the latest information on the whereabouts of all concerned.

Before he was half through, the Inspector slammed the instrument into its cradle. One of them was among the missing and had been for some time. Cristie Lansing had returned to the penthouse and was alone there, the St. Vrain maid had gone out. And Cristie knew too much—The Scotsman started for the door. His orders were swift, sharp. Among them was a command to Steven Hazard. Hazard hurled himself into the corridor. He was followed in a hurry by Dwyer, the Commissioner and Fernandez. The two heads on the pedestals continued to stare from under closed lids at the emptiness of the big dusky room.

Chapter Twenty-Four
HORRIBLE ADMISSIONS

CRISTIE LANSING was tired. She had been running for ages. She went up one long hill and down another. The road went round and round. She was in a cemetery and it was night. But it wasn't night because there was a gray patch somewhere. Her tooth didn't hurt. There were little circles dancing all about her. The circles had bright spots in the middle of them. They expanded and contracted. One of them was Sara. Only Sara wasn't Sara. She was a voice.

She came out of a circle with violet sparks in the center of it. Sara was calling Steven. Steven—who was Steven? Cristie struggled up a steep bank. She had to reach the top. She was choking. She was going to die. She knew she would die if she didn't reach the top. Sara's voice was a rope. The rope was looped around her. It kept dragging her back and down. "Steven, Steven," Sara was saying, "Steven, darling."

Time, time spun an arch. She herself was a tiny figure in the middle of it. The arch receded. She was back in the cemetery again. She was riding at a fast pace. Oh, now she knew. She was asleep and dreaming. In the dream she realized that there was no need to be frightened. She was in a sleigh and the noise that had bothered her, the noise she had heard on the night long ago, the noise the nocturnal visitor had made coming in or going out of Margot St. Vrain's house was the noise of horses, horses with jingling harness on. She was riding behind the running horses.

No, that was silly. She wasn't riding behind them at all, she was on one. It was a big black horse. The jingling was close, loud. She crouched lower, the horse was rearing under her. There was a waterfall somewhere and the dark lip of a cliff. Water, water, there weren't any trees around. Long heath, brown furze. What did it mean, why did she think of that? The horse was galloping now, faster and faster. Her body hurt, her hands and shoulders ached. The horse was running away with her, running straight out toward the lip of the cliff. Her feet were bumping against a floor.

How odd. She was annoyed. The toes of her pumps would be scuffed. Funny to find a rug in the forest. No, it wasn't a rug, it was smooth and cold. One of her pumps fell off. The water was louder now. The horse's harness jingled fiercely. The edge of the cliff was very near. The water cascaded loudly. It filled her ears, went down inside of her body. She gasped for breath. She was on a stage. The stage was back at school. It was Shakespeare, *The Tempest,* something about *The Tempest.* All the lights went out.

She stumbled and hit her head. It was a quotation she was trying to remember. She got it. "Fain would I die a dry death." The horse leaped into midair. She was over the edge of the cliff. She was falling and falling and falling. The water was there, below her, a deep black sea. A sob caught in her throat. She was going to die. She was. She was! Thunderous echoes rang as the water closed over her.

Die a dry death. Fain would I die a dry death. The water was in her now. It was a part of her. She struggled to throw it off. She had to get up out of it, had to get into the air. She threshed her limbs, struck out. Her strength was fading. The blackness came closer.

She tried to tear her head free. It was no use. A gigantic hoof, the jingle of harness again, it wasn't a hoof, it was a hand that pressed her down and down into those black smothering depths. Cristie sighed and lay still.

The high scream of the siren rose and fell as the Cadillac slewed around the corner into Sixty-fourth Street on two wheels. The journey from the gray building on Center Street to the door of the St. Vrain apartment house took seven minutes flat instead of the normal fifteen or twenty.

McKee didn't wait for the radio patrol hustling in from neighboring sectors in response to the alarm from Headquarters.

He was out of the car and across the pavement with Hazard, Dwyer, the Commissioner, Fernandez, and the man at the wheel behind him. The superintendent, two or three bellboys and a knot of excited tenants rushed forward as the group of officials entered the lobby.

McKee left the chauffeur at the main door, shoved the superintendent into the self-service elevator in front of him. The car shot upward with its passengers.

The superintendent's fingers were shaking when he opened the door of Margot St. Vrain's penthouse at the Scotsman's direction. The foyer was empty. So was the living room. Steven Hazard's voice calling, "Cristie, Cristie," didn't get any answer.

The Inspector stood still in the middle of the living room. The odor of chloroform was heavy on the warm air. Two doors opened out of the living room. They were closed. Seconds were important. A wasted fragment of one might be fatal. He heard it thinly as he listened, the soft splash and gurgle. He found the door to Margot St. Vrain's bedroom, darted along a short hall and threw open another door on the right.

The room was a bathroom. The light was on. Cristie Lansing was slumped over the edge of the low tub. She was half in and half out of it. The upper part of her body was hidden. It was bent double. The head and shoulders were inside the tub and the tub was full of water, water that was running faster than the waste pipe could carry it off.

McKee swooped. His arms went round the girl's motionless figure. He called directions to the group of stunned spectators behind him. He lifted Cristie Lansing in his arms, looked down at her. Her face was faintly blue and her eyes were closed. There was a bruise on one temple. No breath was perceptible between her parted lips. They were blue.

Dwyer and the Commissioner helped. They had to restrain Steven Hazard by force. He was frantic. Dwyer swore at him. First aid: the girl's limp body was placed on an ottoman, face down. Flex the arms, send them back and forth, mechanically, steadily, in an attempt to restore respiration. Oxygen had been sent for. Before it came, Cristie Lansing moved. A faint breath stirred her throat and her eyelids fluttered.

McKee didn't wait for the outcome. One of the girl's shoes was off and an attempt had been made to drag·the silk blouse over her head. The attempt had been given up. His mind ranged swiftly. The smell of the chloroform in the living room was still strong although the window there was open. Whoever had attacked Cristie Lansing had been in the penthouse very shortly before their arrival.

Miller downstairs at the main door. The radio cars had·

arrived. Miller had had his instructions. But they were up against a quick-witted and a completely unscrupulous perpetrator. Before the block could be surrounded there was the off-chance of an escape. The perpetrator hadn't gone down in the elevator, that means the stairs. McKee took them in long racing leaps. He drew a blank, emerged in the basement. A white-faced laundress could give him no information. She hadn't seen anyone. McKee dashed on.

Around a turn, through a door. Parcel and storage rooms, both were empty. He threw open the door of the furnace room—and found her.

The quickness of his pursuit had cut off her retreat. She tried to hide. The Inspector saw a fold of her skirt beyond the swelling bulk of a small auxiliary boiler. He said softly, "Don't move, Miss Dodd, stay just where you are," and walked slowly forward.

Mary Dodd talked. After a while they tried to stop her. It couldn't be done. A statement was taken from her in the inner office on the third floor of the Tenth Precinct on West Twentieth Street to which she had been brought directly from the apartment house on Sixty-fourth Street. She attempted no resistance. A single long stare during that first moment of exposure was all. It was a moment in which the soul of the woman seemed to blaze up and be consumed. Afterward she accompanied them without protest, almost with indifference, moving easily and obediently, the shell of a tall, dignified, well-dressed woman going somewhere on an errand that was neither pleasant nor the reverse.

Before he left the Sixty-fourth Street apartment McKee made a swift trip to the penthouse. Cristie Lansing was alive and the probability was that she was going to continue to live. But she was very ill and in a state of shock. Fernandez was looking after her. Steven Hazard knelt on the other side of the bed. Elsewhere in the penthouse were detectives, photographing, recording, examining, for what was to come later.

Back at the Homicide Squad, McKee, Kent, Todhunter, and District Attorney Dwyer listened to Mary Dodd's story.

A bland, almost childlike, expression was on the face she turned to the group of men. Except for her eyes, which were burning and yet dull. They weren't fastened on any one person in the room but on other things, dreadful things beyond its confines. Dwyer was not a sensitive man, but even he was appalled at the sudden flood of invective which poured steadily from the well-cut lips at stated intervals in that long and remarkably coherent narrative.

Mary Dodd had been in love with Steven Hazard for a long time before Sara's death. She had thought in those days that Steven was turning to her. She knew he hated Sara. Then Steven decided to go to South America and Sara decided to go with him. She wouldn't be able to see Steven any more, couldn't be with him. She couldn't bear that. On the night of Margot St. Vrain's party she heard the news. She made up her mind to kill Sara there and then. Then she could go to South America with Steven. She would go anywhere Steven wanted to go. She didn't know about Cristie Lansing at that time, didn't know Steven cared for her.

As McKee listened, he began to realize the thing he had felt all along without being able to isolate or spot—Mary Dodd's absorption, her terrific concentration. It was bent on one object, gratification, a gratification that had been repeatedly denied her. What had really happened was that the love she had borne her dead fiancé had been transferred in part to her father, and on her father's death, to Steven Hazard.

Steven Hazard had become the be-all and end-all of her existence. He was very fond of her. This fondness she had translated into passion. She knew Steven Hazard hated Sara.

Once he had told her that he was going to South America and that Sara was going with him, and in telling, had shown his frustration and despair, Sara Hazard was doomed. Unfortunately, Steven had refrained, during that brief moment at Margot St. Vrain's party, from telling Mary Dodd why he was so overwhelmed.

She, poor creature, had thought it was simply hatred for Sara and a desire for a different life that might include her. . . . The rest was self-evident. The dignified woman kept on talking.

She waited outside the penthouse, saw Sara's encounter with Pat, saw Euen Firth take Sara home. She followed the cream-colored roadster to Franklin Place. When she was within a block of the Hazard apartment, she thought she saw Sara coming toward her. It wasn't Sara. It was the maid, Eva Prentice, wearing Sara's clothes.

She, Mary, continued on her way. When she was half a block from the apartment house door Sara came out and turned the corner and got into the Hazard car parked at the curb near the top of the hill. She got into the car with Sara. She said she was worried about Steven, asked Sara to drive her home.

Sara wasn't suspicious. Her black velvet bag with the gun in it was on the seat between them. Mary Dodd managed to get the gun out without Sara's seeing her. She

knew Sara was carrying it around with her. She distracted
Sara's attention, made her turn, and hit her with the butt
of the automatic. Sara fell forward over the wheel.

Mary Dodd turned the ignition key and started the motor.
She released the brake, put the car in high, let in the clutch
and stepped out on the running board. As the car got
under way she advanced the throttle and jumped.

The car went down the hill and into the river. Mary
Dodd said she watched it go from a dark alley between two
buildings on the side street. She saw Cristie Lansing run
by the mouth of the alley. After a few minutes she herself
went home.

She killed the maid Eva Prentice on September 11th.
Mary Dodd described the second killing in the same dreadful detail. The day after Sara's death, the day that the story
of the car crash was in the papers, Eva Prentice called her
up. Eva demanded money. Mary Dodd knew that the maid
suspected her because of their encounter on the street just
before Sara went into the river. She paid Eva a thousand
dollars on account. The maid was a thief herself and was
hiding out in the Twenty-first Street room.

Mary went there several times. It was during the third
visit that she killed Eva. She knew she would never have
any freedom while Eva was alive, that Eva might tell Steven
and Steven wouldn't marry her. Eva might also tell the
police and she might be electrocuted.

Eva had demanded ten thousand dollars from her. Mary
Dodd went to the room on Twenty-first Street at seven
o'clock on the night of the 11th of September. She told
Eva that she hadn't that much money, but that she expected
it during the evening. She said that the maid could go back
with her to her house and wait for it, if she wanted to. Eva

agreed to this.

She went behind the screen in the corner of the room on Twenty-first Street to wash her face and put on her make-up. Mary followed her, hit her over the head with a heavy brass paper-weight that had belonged to her father and that she had brought with her as a weapon, if one should be necessary.

The maid fell forward against the wall. Mary pushed her head down into the water in the wash basin. Eva Prentice struggled but Mary held her under until she stopped struggling. Then she wiped her face, dried her hair and put her hat on.

Her own car was waiting in front of the door. She realized the danger, but she had to take a chance. She put her arm around Eva, put Eva's arm around her own shoulder. The hall was empty. She managed to get the maid out into the areaway and up the three steps. A man stopped on the pavement and said, "Need help, lady?" Mary said, "No, thanks," her friend had had a little too much to drink but that she could manage. The man walked on.

Mary got Eva into her car. She drove up to Kokino. She knew the place well. She had thought and thought of some way in which to hide the maid's body so that it would never again be found. She and Sara and Steven had swum in the cove beside the point many times. Steven had shown them the rock fissures at the side of the deep pool.

When she got to Kokino she took off her clothes. The water wasn't cold. She put a rope around Eva's body, got her down, shoved her deep into a crevice, slipped off the rope, smoothed away all traces on the bank above, re-dressed herself and returned to New York.

No one suspected anything. Sara's body was recovered

and identified and buried. She saw Steven on and off during those days. Steven said nothing, but she was content to wait. And then one evening she went to Margot St. Vrain's with him to hear a new song and she discovered that Steven was in love with Cristie Lansing. She opened the door of a room and found them alone together with their arms around each other.

At that point another stream of dreadful, quiet obscenity poured from Mary Dodd's lips. It went on for a long while. When they brought her to a halt, she answered questions monotonously, like a person in a hypnotic trance.

She was the writer of the anonymous note that had turned up on McKee's desk on the day following his return from Rio. There was no doubt of her motive. She made it quite clear. She hated Steven Hazard as much as she had formerly loved him, hated Cristie Lansing with an even deeper hatred, wanted to keep them apart, wanted to see one or both of them suffer the death penalty for the murder she had committed.

At that time she still had the gun with which she had knocked Sara out. She knew its possession was a menace to her. She told the Inspector the truth—that Sara had stolen it—in order to pave the way for her next step—which was to implicate Steven and also Cristie. She wrote to Steve, signing Eva Prentice's name, and demanded a thousand dollars for her silence about Cristie's having been on the scene the night Sara was killed. She told Steven to send it to general delivery.

The envelope was already lying on McKee's desk. Mary Dodd explained that she had never tried to collect it. She didn't want the money. She still had the gun. She had slipped it into her pocket on the night she killed Sara, afraid to leave it in the car with her fingerprints on it. She had no time then to wipe them off. She had kept the gun for fear that if she simply threw it away it might be traced to her. She decided to get rid of the weapon by placing it in Steven's hands under incriminating circumstances. She had sent him a second letter telling him to go to Eva's room on Twenty-first Street, telling him exactly where the gun was. At the same time she sent a note to Cristie Lansing so that Cristie would be there when Steven arrived. She knew Steven was being followed, felt sure that the police would find them both there with the gun.

It didn't work out precisely as she had planned it. A little frown etched itself on her smooth white forehead. She went on talking.

The night that McKee played the record of the talk between Sara and Cliff, the germ for resuscitating Sara came to her. She was aware that records had been made of the voices of various guests at Margot St. Vrain's party. Sara was among the people who had been recorded.

She decided that if she could only make Steven believe that Sara was alive, if she could make him believe that it was the maid, Eva Prentice, whose body he had identified and that Cristie Lansing had killed Eva in mistake for Sara, everything would be quite easy and simple.

Earlier, much earlier, on the night she saw Cristie in Steven's arms, she had decided to kill Cristie when she got round to it. That was the night on which she slipped a spare key from Margot St. Vrain's ring. When she returned to the living room, she saw Margot's key-ring lying on a table. Cristie worked in the penthouse alone during the day. The key offered access to her if she, Mary, should need it.

When she decided to try to impersonate Sara by reproducing her voice, the first thing she had to do was get hold of the record. She knew that Margot was away. She entered the penthouse secretly, late at night. She found the record in the cabinet. She had to take several others to make sure she had the right one. While she was in the living room, Cristie Lansing woke up and called out. She managed to get away undetected.

The next day she bought a machine that would play the record with Sara's voice on it. She practiced for hours, whenever she got the chance. She knew that if the plan was to succeed it would have to be well done. There were other voices besides Sara's on the record. She had to find the spot where Sara began and ended, had to learn to manipulate the lever so as to cut it off at the proper moment. It was very difficult but she finally got it right.

She knew that there was something going on between Steven and Cristie Lansing, knew they were planning something and that she had to act quickly. She was familiar with Steven's routine. The week-end stretched ahead. She called him after lunch on that Saturday at his club.

Steven answered. She switched on the record. She played the best bit of Sara, the only bit that fitted her purpose. "Hello, Steven. Having a good time, darling?" Sara always called people darling when she wanted to be particularly nasty. As soon as the word "darling" was finished, Mary Dodd said she had switched off the lever and had placed a handkerchief over the mouthpiece. She dropped her voice and gave the rest of her message in a whisper as though there was someone near her and she couldn't talk very loud.

The trick worked. Steven believed that it was Sara on the other end of the phone, that Sara wasn't dead. He agreed to do as he was told. She was very pleased for a while and then worried again.

She was afraid that in spite of the warning Steven and Cristie might get together. She didn't want them to match stories. It was she who had sent the telegram to Steven at Kokino, the telegram telling him to be out on the point that night and to bring a thousand dollars with him. He went. She pretended to go to bed and slipped out a side door of the farmhouse. When she got out on the point, she saw Steven dimly, silhouetted against the waters of the lake. She didn't go anywhere near him, had no intention of doing so. What she meant to do was to establish herself as Sara by throwing Sara's gold compact, which she had taken from among her things when she was packing them, into the bushes near Steven. After that she meant to slip away without being seen.

The fictitious interruption she had planned became real. Just as she was about to call to Steven she collided with somebody on the edge of the bank fifty feet from where Steven stood. The person, whoever it was, let out a cry and started to grapple with her. She, Mary, had shoved. The person toppled and dislodged a boulder. Whoever the intruder was, she screamed and fell. The dislodged stone rolled down the bank and fell into the lake with a loud splash. Mary had run quickly back toward the house. When she was half way along the path she heard someone running toward her. She faced about and pretended to be making for the point. The man coming toward her was a detective. He took her back to the farmhouse with him.

She admitted quite calmly that she was pleased with her work on Halloween night. Her only fear, and it was soon allayed, was that the police would find Eva Prentice's body.

It wasn't until yesterday, Friday, that she learned the truth, that Eva's body had been discovered and brought up by Steven.

She still wasn't particularly frightened. She felt sure that neither Sara's body nor the maid's was in any condition to be identified. Dwyer, Kent and Todhunter took a quick glance at the Inspector. The Scotsman said nothing. His face was drawn, sad. He kept on watching Mary Dodd. She continued to recount events in that toneless flowing voice.

That afternoon she had become really frightened for the first time. Cristie Lansing had shown signs of remembering something, something important, in the meeting at Pat Somers's.

Mary Dodd knew her carefully built security was threatened. She couldn't let that girl get away with it. She had to take steps. It was her dog Winkie who showed her the way. Winkie was paralyzed and had to be put out of his misery. She had to kill Winkie herself in the middle of the preceding summer, with chloroform. There was still a lot of chloroform in the bottle.

As soon as Cristie Lansing left Pat's she telephoned to the penthouse. She wanted to get Cristie alone there. Margot St. Vrain was going back to her office, but she had to get rid of Margot's maid. She told the girl that she was delivering a message for Miss St. Vrain and that Miss St. Vrain wanted the maid to meet her at Grand Central right away with an overnight bag at the Information Booth.

She went home and got the record and the chloroform. It took her only a few minutes. She went to the penthouse. At that point Mary Dodd's voice began to fail, not from strain and not from remorse; fury choked it, fury at the defeat of her last desperate gesture, the details of which they knew.

Horror thickened within the walls of the room as the black current poured out. Todhunter shrank in his chair. Dwyer and McKee said nothing. There was nothing to say. Kent went on busily recording.

Chapter Twenty-Five
A FINAL TOAST

THE FIELD COMMANDER was very kind. When McKee arrived at La Guardia Airport he found that the office had been swept and garnished and was at his disposal. McKee stood at one of the windows and watched landing planes beyond the long esplanade taxiing up and disgorging passengers in the November afternoon sunlight.

A week had passed since the wind-up of the Hazard-Prentice case. Dwyer had asked for and had obtained two first-degree indictments against Mary Elizabeth Dodd of East Seventy-third Street, New York City, for the murders of Sara Hazard and Eva Prentice.

The door opened and the couple for whom he was waiting came in. The girl who had been Cristie Lansing turned a quiet face toward the Scotsman. Her hand was on Steven Hazard's elbow. Hazard looked tired but there was peace in his face too, peace and the foreshadowing of happiness. He and Cristie Lansing had been married that morning. They were taking a plane south.

There were no attendants, no bridesmaids, no other guests at that impromptu farewell party with the exception of Pat Somers who followed them into the room. Behind him two uniformed waiters pushed in service tables.

Pat was beaming. His benevolent glance included the Scotsman. He directed the waiters, fussed over the food, the wine, uncorked the Pol Roget himself.

"You can't beat this," he said, settling back expansively in the inadequate chair, "and by God, McKee, when it comes right down to it, you can't beat you either."

The Scotsman bowed his thanks. Cristie and Steven raised their glasses. For a moment Cristie's eyes were full of tears. She winked them out of existence. Laughter, then, and talk and more champagne. They had to get down to it in the end. It was Pat and Steven who put those final questions.

Pat began it. He said soberly, "Steven, old man, I want to apologize for the crack Cliff took at you that day in the Commissioner's office when he told the Inspector here to ask you about the gun Sara had stolen from Mary Dodd's. Cliff just lost his head."

Steven waved the incident away.

McKee said drily, "Your brother wasn't the only one, Pat. It so often happens that way. Look at Margot St. Vrain. It was Margot St. Vrain who collided with Mary Dodd in the darkness of the point up there in Kokino on Halloween. Margot was on her way to meet you, Pat, when she ran into Mary Dodd. It was Margot who screamed that night. She and Euen Firth and Johnny were all in the vicinity of the point and they all tried to cover up.

"Incidentally we got hold of Mrs. Thompson yesterday. As we had previously ascertained, she isn't really Mrs. Thompson. It doesn't matter now. Margot St. Vrain paid the woman a sum of money to disappear so that no embarrassing questions would be asked. Mrs. Thompson took a plane to Miami and cabled Thompson from there to keep his mouth shut and join her."

"What," Pat demanded, "has become of that ass Firth?"

Cristie helped herself to salad. "Euen isn't actually such

an ass," she said. "He's not a bad fellow underneath that manner. He's not too bright but he does love Margot. He was worried about her all the time, that's why he kept trailing people around, why he went over to the point Halloween. He was trying to find out what was wrong. The funny part of it was Margot needn't have worried. It's going to work out all right. She's going to get a divorce, she's talked it out with Euen's father and mother and they've been lambs."

Steven took a sip of champagne and shook his head. His face clouded over. He said, "I don't like to talk about it at a time like this, but I can't help thinking of it, Inspector, and it bothers me. Why did Mary Dodd take such an awful chance at the end, why did she risk a telephone call to me when I was actually down there in the Commissioner's office at Headquarters?"

McKee said, "I can answer that because I put the question to her myself. Up to the very last she wanted to maintain the fiction that your wife was still alive. According to her reckoning, all we had were two unidentifiable bodies. She didn't know," he hesitated, "about the Hoffman test, about what Fernandez had managed to do. She wanted to fasten her existence firmly on you until her end was accomplished. She intended to leave something of Sara's in the St. Vrain apartment just as she had left the compact on the point. She also intended, as you know, to kill Miss Lansing."

There was a small cold pause.

"It was a desperate thing to do," the Scotsman continued, "but Miss Dodd knew she had to try to drive her point home.

Her state of mind at that point was pretty edgy. If Miss Lansing's death looked like accident, well and good. If not,

she hoped your former wife would be marked as the crim-
inal. From that day on she would have disappeared out of
existence. Miss Dodd broke the record; we found the re-
mains of it in the fireplace in the penthouse."

"You never suspected Sara's voice was a record, Steve?"
Pat asked.

Steven said no. It had sounded so like her, not merely
her voice, which she kept low and covered after the first
few words, but the things she said. She had warned him
to keep away from Cristie, not to communicate with her
in any way. His fear had paralyzed his wits, obscured his
judgment. He simply didn't dare to take the slightest
chance. That was what had made him attempt that fright-
ful experiment off Kokino—to get, out of the whole terrible puzzle, some certain knowledge. He had no idea of
who or what had gone into the water. Sara might have had
an accomplice. He had to try and find out. . . .

Cristie's fingers touched his sleeve. His hand covered hers.

An airline attendant opened the door, thrust in his head.
He said, "Ship will be ready in a few minutes," and withdrew.

Cristie rose, gathered her purse and gloves. Steven rose
with her and they walked off in opposite directions to
dressing rooms.

Pat looked at the Scotsman. He said, "Well, you certainly got the angles on this case, McKee, but there are still
a couple of them I haven't caught up with. I know that
Cliff and Kit crossed each other up about being in the
living room up there in the Hazard farmhouse when they
were really roaming around outside watching each other.
But here's what I don't get. What about that fellow Loomis,
Eva Prentice's boy friend? What made Cristie think that

Steven took the gun out of the pocket of Sara's fur cape on the night of Margot's party—and what was it that Cristie was about to spill in my office just before she was attacked?"

McKee balanced a salted almond on his thumb nail. "Loomis is out of the picture. He was never in it. We finally located him. The last time he saw Eva Prentice was late on the night that Sara Hazard was killed. The maid met him in that room in Twenty-first Street. They had a few hours together and then Loomis lit out.

"As far as the gun and Sara Hazard are concerned, Sara took it from the Dodd house originally because she was playing a dangerous game and wanted to be armed and ready. She was shifting the gun about a lot on the evening of Margot's party. I've talked to a number of people. She had it in her purse when she arrived. She didn't want to lug it around. She put it into her fur cape pocket later, after her visit to Cliff. When the party began to thin, she put it back in her purse. I suppose she didn't want whoever helped her on with her cape to know she was toting a weapon.

"As for Cristie Lansing's memory. As a matter of fact she didn't remember anything at all. What actually happened was that seated in your office and while she was thinking of something else she caught a glimpse of Mary Dodd in an attitude she didn't recognize and couldn't connect up. Nevertheless that subconscious fragment made her quite sure that Steven was not the person who had jumped off the running board of the car as Sara went down the hill to her death in the East River. Anything else you'd like to know?"

Pat nodded. He said, "Yes, I want to know whether you knew when you left Headquarters that day who the killer was?"

The Scotsman said, "I'm not proud of my knowledge. It gave that girl in there," he waved toward the dressing room, "a pretty risky time. Yes, I knew. Once Mary Dodd got Headquarters and Steven Hazard, she thought she was safe. She didn't expect anyone to cut in. I did. I took the receiver from Hazard. Just before she hung up I heard a sound."

He paused. Steven and Cristie were coming toward him.

"Remember your little horses," he said to the girl, "your little horses and not twinkle, twinkle, but tinkle, tinkle. Mary Dodd has an antique silver bracelet with little primitives, real primitives, hanging from it. She wears the bracelet almost constantly. She wore it on the night she entered Margot St. Vrain's apartment and removed the record. Had a pony, did you, when you were a kid?"

Cristie gave him a surprised "Yes."

The Scotsman went on. "The tinkle reminded you of harness. It was really a three-cornered sound. I heard it first as a soft chime the day she told me about the gun. You heard it next as your little horses. I heard it over the telephone in Headquarters as a combination of the two. The result added up to murder. As soon as the tail on her reported that she was at the penthouse, I knew, and I realized where we were."

Pat Somers said, "And a damn good thing too," and emptied the remainder of the bottle into the glasses for a final toast. All four drank it standing.

Outside on the edge of the field Pat and McKee kissed the bride. Steven and Cristie went one way, Pat and the Scotsman waited. The two men stood side by side on the esplanade looking down. Mr. and Mrs. Steven Hazard mounted the incline. They paused at the top, waved and then disappeared.

The door of the ship closed. The idling motors rose to a higher note. The plane moved. It taxied to the head of the runway, stood poised for a few moments, roared down the runway and bounced once or twice. Then it pulled itself into the air, began to mount and swung west into the setting sun.

FEB 1 5 2019

CPSIA information can be obtained
at www.ICGtesting.com
Printed in the USA
LVHW041446070119
603020LV00001B/33/P